W9-AFU-891

Apples from Heaven

NAOMI BALTUCK

APPLES FROM HEAVEN

Multicultural Folk Tales About Stories and Storytellers

LINNET BOOKS

1995

First published 1995 as a Linnet Book,
an imprint of The Shoe String Press, Inc.,
North Haven, Connecticut 06473.

Library of Congress Cataloging-in-Publication Data

Baltuck, Naomi, 1956–
Apples from heaven : multicultural folk tales about stories and storytellers / by Naomi Baltuck.
p. cm.
Includes bibliographical references and index.
Summary: A collection of international folk tales about storytelling and the role of stories in transmitting information, history, and values.
ISBN 0-208-02424-7 (cloth: alk. paper).
ISBN 0-208-02434-4 (paper: alk. paper)
1. Folklore—Cross-cultural studies—Juvenile literature.
2. Folklore—Study and teaching—Juvenile literature.
3. Storytelling—Juvenile literature. 4. Multiculturalism—Juvenile literature. [1. Folklore. 2. Storytelling.] I. Title.
GR69.B35 1995
398.2—dc20 95-21890
CIP AC

The paper in this publication meets the
minimum requirements of American National
Standard for Information Sciences—Permanence
of Paper for Printed Library Materials,
ANSI Z39.48–1984. ♾

Designed by Abigail Johnston
Printed in the United States of America

This book is written for my Grandma Rose, my very first storyteller,
and for my mother Eleanor and her mother Rhea,
who used to tell me stories over the kitchen table.
It is for my daughters Eleanor and Beatrice, who even now,
at their tender ages, share stories back and forth over our kitchen table.
It is also for my older sister Deborah, who enthralled her
little sister with her stories of "Fanny Fantastic" and "Egbert Enormous,"
and for Mr. Melamed, the high school history teacher who
turned American history into one long juicy story.
It is for my dear friends and favorite storytellers
Pat Peterson, Sharon Creeden, Margie MacDonald,
and Meg Philp-Paterson, who have made me laugh
and given me so many of the stories I hold in my heart.
And last of all, it is written in loving memory
of Joy Anderson and Beth Jacobsen, who have gone on to the next world,
but left their stories behind to brighten this world for us all.
—N.B.

"When a day passes it is no longer there. What remains of it?
Nothing more than a story. If stories weren't told or
books weren't written, man would live like the beasts—only for the day.
Today we live, but by tomorrow today will be a story.
The whole world, all human life, is one long story."
—Isaac Bashevis Singer

Contents

III. • ONE FOR THE ONE WHO TAKES IT TO HEART

Three apples fell from heaven.
One for the teller,
One for the listener,
And one for the one who took it to heart.
—Armenian folk saying

Introduction

AT THE HEART OF VIRTUALLY EVERY WORLD CULTURE, you will find its stories. Preserved in those stories are the values, the history, the soul of that people. No wonder that throughout time the minstrels and bards, the griots and raconteurs, the skalds and shanachies, have been such valued members of their societies. And while the professionals toured the land and recited their epics before kings, by the fireside grandmothers passed down their tales while carding wool or stirring the porridge.

Our stories connect us with our past, our present, and our future. Due to industrialization, the spread of literacy, and the modern world's infatuation with, or rather addiction to, television, radio, and similar technologies, we were in danger of losing that connection. Indeed, many tales have been lost and forgotten. But as Ernest Rhys, poet, historian, and author, has said, "A fairy-tale, like a cat, has nine lives; it can pass into many queer shapes, and yet not die. You may cut off its head or drown it in sentiment or sea-water, or tie a moral to its tail; but it will survive, and be found sitting safe by the fire some winter night." Far from being dead, storytelling has enjoyed a renaissance. It has been welcomed back from the nursery, to which the tales, carefully watered-down, had been relegated. In the last twenty-five years or so, storytelling has been recognized as essential to the well-being of a society. It is now considered an art as well as a folk art to be taken seriously not only by teachers and performers but by doctors, lawyers, counselors, therapists, educators, ministers, and even scientists.

Like most people, I did not understand how deeply woven our stories are into the fabric of our everyday life. It was not until I became aware of storytelling as an art and had begun to perform professionally that I realized the extent of the power and influence that stories have on our lives. There is a traditional Armenian folk saying, "Three apples fell from heaven; one for the teller, one for the listener, and one for the one who took it to heart." I can now look back and see that even in my infancy I was spoonfed heavenly applesauce. One of the earliest memories I have is of sitting on my Grandma Rose's lap and listening to her tell stories in a soft, low voice seasoned with the tang of the Old Country. As soon as Grandma walked through our door, her seven grandchildren swarmed over her. We would hang on her skirt and vie for a prime position on her lap or beside her on our well-worn couch, with the rest of the kids spilling over to sit at her feet. "Tell us a story, Grandma, from your mouth," we would beg.

Like Ali the Persian, Grandma Rose told both stories that she had heard with her own ears and stories that she had seen with her own eyes as a child growing up in the Ukraine before the turn of the century. I had no idea where the Ukraine was, but I understood what a pogrom was. Vividly I could picture my grandmother as a young Jewish girl, hiding with the rest of her family beneath a mattress covered with coal in the cellar of a friendly Gentile family. Hunched and shivering in the dark, they listened to the screams of the horses, the shouts of the cossacks, the sounds of destruction all around. When Grandma Rose came to the part where her little sister Clara, burning with fever, died in her arms while they huddled in terror, her eyes always filled with tears. And every time she told that story, Grandma would take my face in her hands and say, "You look just like my little Clara."

At five years old, I would listen to that story and know in my heart that I was special to my grandmother. At fifteen, I would listen wide-eyed and thrill at the drama and adventure of it. At twenty-five,

I could feel it tugging at my roots all the way from the Old Country. And at thirty-five, though my grandmother was no longer there to tell it to me, I would think of her story and take comfort in knowing that I was from a family of strong women, survivors. Apples from heaven.

As a primary teacher, storytelling was the apple I gave back to my students. Many doors are opened when a child lets a story come in. Ruth Sawyer, author of *The Way of the Storyteller*, and one who helped to keep the art alive during storytelling's "dark age," said that if we can touch the heart, then the head will understand. We have in storytelling a key which opens the doors to many disciplines. I used it to teach creative writing, movement and dance, history, social studies, science and geography, problem-solving, and vocabulary.

But it was much more than a teaching tool. I wished that every morning I could have had each student climb up into my lap for ten minutes of my undivided attention. Yet with so many children and all the demands and constraints of maintaining a classroom, it was impossible to spend as much time with each individual child as I would have liked. I used storytelling to build bridges and fill in the gaps. Lewis Carroll once called stories "love gifts." My students understood this instinctively every time we pushed back the desks for story time. Whether I began my story with "Once upon a time . . ." or "When I was a kid . . . ," each child seemed to feel that I was bestowing that "love gift" upon her especially. Relationships changed. A fertile atmosphere was created in which trust and affection were nurtured both in the storyteller and her listeners. More apples from heaven.

They say an apple a day keeps the doctor away. Unfortunately, that is not true. But I have found that an apple from heaven can be as good as a trip to the doctor, and cheaper than therapy. In 1989, my mother lost a long and painful battle with cancer. I returned to my childhood home in Detroit to live with her and nurse her through the last months of her life. I had never witnessed such suffering. After she died, I could not blot out the ugly memories of her pain. And then there were my own crushed hopes to contend with. I had dreamed of taking her to Europe. I had wanted to give her grandchildren. I longed to see her hold my babies in her arms and give them her blessing. I searched for some way to deal with the hurt and loss and disappointment. Then I remembered: *I am a storyteller.* Somewhere out there was a story that I could learn, feel, tell, and that would heal me.

The holidays, always a difficult time for the bereaved, drew near. I began to seek out fresh holiday material. During the daylight hours, I read folk and fairy tales and at night, after I had gone to bed, I lay awake recalling Christmases from my own past. Bit by bit, they began to shape themselves into a story of one particular Christmas at the Baltuck house, with my mother and brothers and sisters all prominent characters. After many nights, the story had gelled to the point where I could tell it to myself as I was going to sleep. One night, soon after that, my mother came to me in a dream. In my dream, she was helping me "re-arrange" my new life without her, right down to the furniture in the house I had just moved to. And before she left me, my mother gave me cookies for later. I woke with a calm sense of well-being.

When I shared my family Christmas story with an audience for the first time, it was very well-received. My audience felt good, I felt good, and I knew that I had cleared, if not the last, then the highest hurdle in the way of my own recovery. I had moved forward by moving backward to happier times.

That holiday story was the first of many family stories that I now tell. Like the old woman in the story, "Tell It to the Walls," I used storytelling to knock down the walls of my sorrow. Once the scars began to heal, I found that I was using stories to explore other issues in my life, such as coming of age, loss, risk-taking, self-reliance, and motherhood. Internalizing and telling the traditional folk and fairy tales was as effective to the healing process as telling my own family stories. I once spoke to a storyteller who told me that a story she had told a hundred times about a selkie—a seal child who comes to a childless couple, grows up, and returns to the sea—had taken on a new and deeper meaning for her now that her own daughter was preparing to leave home and go out into the world on her own.

They say that an apple never falls far from the tree. I discovered in the most wonderful way that this can be true for heavenly apples as well. Last year, as I was combing and braiding my three-year-old daughter Eleanor's hair, I told her, "When I was your age, my favorite part of the day was when my mother used to brush and braid my hair each morning." Without thinking, I added, "I wish you could have known your Grandma Eleanor."

But my daughter replied, "I DO know her, Mama. Will you tell me about the time Grandma Eleanor took you up the mountain?"

When I heard those words, I realized once again the power of stories. Through them, my daughter had come to know and love the grandmother she had never met. And now, when Eleanor climbs up into my lap and says to me, "Tell me a story, Mama, from your mouth," I know that I have been blessed with apples from heaven.

Because we are human, you, as well as I, have partaken of all three apples from heaven; they are a part of the minimum daily requirement of heart's ease, soul's delight, and food for thought. This book is a collection of traditional world folk tales and proverbs that celebrate both story and storyteller. The stories, coming from lands as diverse as America and Africa, are sweet and bittersweet, heart-warming and spine-tingling, thought-provoking and rib-tickling, and they defy the barriers of time, geography, and politics. Here you will find the stories of liars, boasters, and braggarts who live to tell, as well as the story of the man with no story. Though you have not met, you will smile in recognition at the antics of Little Bobtail. And though it may have been at another time and place, you too have been moved to tears by a sweet, tragic tale like that of Donn Bó.

And so this book is for anyone who tells stories, whether it is to teach, to heal, or to entertain. It is for those who love to listen as well. But most of all, it is for those who take the stories to heart. Apples from heaven fall everywhere. Catch them as they fall. Take a bite; pass them on; plant their seeds and watch them grow. Apples from heaven.

I

ONE FOR THE TELLER

"All the world is on the tip of the tongue."
—Jewish folk saying

The Golden Lamb

[IRAQ]

DURING THE DAYS OF CALIPH HARUN AL-RASHID, there lived three young men who were fast friends. They all decided to set out together and seek their fortunes. But in order to earn money with which to begin their travels, they agreed to spend the winter tending sheep for an old widow.

"These are hungry times," she told them. "I cannot pay you in coin, but if you work for me until lambing season is over, you may have your choice of the new lambs."

The three young men agreed. All winter long they tended the flock, and spun grand tales of the rich lives they would one day lead. In the spring, many lambs were born. But one of them was a wondrous lamb, born with a golden fleece. The old woman told them, "I promised a lamb to each of you. Golden or no, the lamb is yours and you are welcome to it. But you must decide among yourselves which of you shall get the golden lamb."

Of course, each of the three friends wanted that lamb, for such a rarity would fetch a good price at the market and provide more than enough coins to begin a journey and a new life. They debated the matter to no avail until finally one of them suggested, "Let us go to Baghdad. When we get to the city, we will take this dispute to Caliph

Harun al-Rashid himself, for he is said to be a wise and just man. Let him decide which of us deserves the golden lamb."

The three young men set out for Baghdad with the golden lamb. All the way to the gates of the city, they argued over which of the three was the most deserving. When they were ushered into the presence of so great a man, their knees trembled beneath their robes. Still they found the courage to explain their problem.

"I should get the lamb, Your Honor," said the first of the three, "for I am the eldest. Are we not taught from childhood to respect our elders? What better sign of respect than to allow me to have the lamb?"

"But I am the most clever," said the second, "and could put the money to best use."

"Ah," said the third, "but I have a widowed mother and many young brothers and sisters to provide for. Would that not be a noble cause to support?"

When they had finished, the caliph remained silent for a moment. At last he said, "There is no doubt that this is a difficult decision, made even more difficult since you have each stated your case most eloquently. It is apparent that you are each blessed with a gift for words, so I shall let that be the deciding factor. You shall each tell a story to me and my courtiers. He who tells the best tale shall be proclaimed winner and receive as his reward the golden lamb."

One of the three friends stepped forward and said, "If it please Your Magnificence, I shall share the first story." He began with a story of an adventurer's daring quest. As his tale unfolded, the young man wove a spell of enchantment over the entire audience. He regaled the royal courtiers, who listened awestruck to the exploits of the brave young hero. At last his quest was fulfilled and the world made right again. When the young storyteller was finished, the audience sat dumbstruck, still caught up in the excitement of the tale.

"Excellent!" exclaimed Caliph Harun al-Rashid. "That is a tale that will be difficult to equal."

The second of the three friends stepped forward and said, "I shall live up to the challenge, Omnipotent One." He then proceeded to work a very different kind of story magic. In a voice as smooth as silk, the young man told a heartwarming tale of love lost and found. All present in the court felt their hearts ache with loneliness and then soar like eagles when two star-crossed lovers were finally reunited for all time. When the storyteller finished, there wasn't a dry eye among the listeners and the air was filled with the soft sighs of the ladies.

"Superb!" cried the caliph. "But there is yet one more story to hear."

"O Most Magnanimous One, I hope that if my offering is last, it shall not be least," said the third young man as he stepped forward and bowed. Then he began a story, not of adventure or love, but of mystery and suspense. The audience was so caught up in the thrill of the story, they forgot to breathe. The young teller led them on a journey through a tangled line of plot and counter-plot shrouded in darkness. At the conclusion, like a conjuror, he laid open a final astounding revelation and the crowd burst into applause and loud cheers.

Only the caliph sat in silence. He frowned and tugged at his beard. At last, he said, "Step forward."

The three friends obeyed and nervously awaited the judgment of that great man. Finally the caliph said, "Before I make a final decision, I would have you each answer one more question. Were I to award you the lamb, what would you do with the fortune you received from the sale of it?"

The first young man replied, "I would rent a stall in the market, Your Magnificence, and open a shop. I could sell silks and spices and, in time, I would be rich."

"And you?" asked the caliph of the second young man.

"I would use my money to learn to keep accounts. Then I could work for a rich merchant and thereby make my place in the world."

"And you?" the caliph asked of the third young man.

"I would travel abroad and bring back rare merchandise to sell at a profit. Then I would use the proceeds to buy more wares. Before long, my fortune would be made."

The caliph nodded thoughtfully. Then he declared, "The stories you told were of equal value, though each was different and each special in its own way. I have therefore decided to take the lamb and divide it equally three ways. Is that acceptable to you all?"

"But Your Magnificence," said one of the young men, "we have already agreed among ourselves that one of us would receive all the profits. In that way, at least one shall have the means of making his fortune in the world. To divide it into three parts would mean that none of us would have sufficent funds to make good use of."

"I promise you," the caliph assured them, "that you shall each have what you need to begin a rewarding new life."

The three friends had no choice; the caliph would divide the spoils as he saw most fitting. Perhaps, they reasoned, a golden lamb might still bring a high enough price to finance three new starts in the world.

They watched the caliph whisper into the ear of his vizier. The vizier bowed to the caliph and left the hall. The three young men anxiously waited for his return. Would he bring them gold? Silver? Jewels?

At last the vizier returned with arms laden. At the feet of each of the three young men the caliph's vizier placed a warm cloak, a sturdy pair of sandals, and a loaf of bread.

At first the young men could only stare dumbly at the caliph's settlement. Then one of them stammered, "What of our money, my lord?"

"I never promised you money," the caliph replied. "I only promised you what you would need, and that is exactly what I have given you."

"What good are these things to us?" they cried in dismay.

"The sandals will carry you far," replied the caliph. "The cloaks will protect you from the chill of night. The bread will nourish you on your journey until you reach your next destination. And once you arrive, the people there will gladly fulfill your every need."

"In exchange for what?" asked all three in bewilderment. "We have no trade to practice and, without the money from the golden lamb, we have no goods to sell. What can we possibly offer them?"

"Why your marvelous stories, of course!" smiled the caliph. "If I were to give you money for the golden lamb, what would you do with it? You would become merchants and accountants. There is a place in the world for such as these. But if any one of you were to follow that path, it would be a shameful waste. Clearly the three of you were meant for something else. My friends, in this matter, please harken to my words. Do not mourn for that which you do not possess, but rejoice for the gifts you have been given. Go forth, storytellers, and share your blessed gift with the world."

No sooner had the caliph spoken, than the ladies and gentlemen of the court cheered and stepped forward to offer their encouragement to the three weavers of words. The gentlemen rewarded the storytellers for their magnificent tales by pressing coins into their palms. The ladies gave them sweet treats to eat as they traveled.

And the three young men lived to appreciate the wisdom of Caliph Harun al-Rashid. Together they traveled the width and breadth of the land. Just as the caliph had foretold, wherever they went, they were welcomed, well-fed, and well-cared for in exchange for the pleasure they gave. If they did not amass great fortunes of silver and gold, the three storytellers were rich in friendship and contentment. Most important, they acquired the wisdom to understand the worth of those treasures.

"What can you expect from a pig but a grunt?"
—English folk saying

The Dragon King's Feast

[CHINA]

LONG AGO IN CHINA, there lived two brothers who were both known for their talent as tellers of tall tales. Each was constantly trying to surpass the other in his skill as a storyteller. Though neither brother ever succeeded in fooling the other into believing one of his lies, that didn't stop him from trying. It got so that they couldn't get together without one wild story following on the heels of another.

One day the younger brother went to visit his elder brother, who had recently returned from visiting a relative. As they drank their tea, the elder brother said, "In our cousin's village, there is a temple with a drum so large that the temple rests within the great drum itself. Before they can beat the drum, the temple has to be cleared of people or its boom would surely burst their ears."

"A most unusual drum," observed the younger brother. "While you were away, brother, I too saw a rare sight. A farmer came through our village leading an ox so enormous that even while its head was in our marketplace, its tail was still miles behind in the last village."

"That is ridiculous!" scoffed the elder. "No ox could be that big!"

"If there is no ox so big," observed the younger, "then where did they get the skin for that drum of yours? Admit that you were just trying to fool me with one of your outrageous lies."

"Just so," confessed the elder brother. "Perhaps we have become obsessed with this perversion. Come, little brother, let us go to the river and wash away this foolish addiction."

The younger brother agreed. But he did not know that his older brother was merely plotting another scheme. When the older brother undressed and dove into the water, he had with him a piece of meat hidden in his hand. He ducked beneath the surface and disappeared from sight. After a short swim, he came wading out of the water, eating the meat in a most conspicuous manner.

"Where did you get that meat, my brother?" asked the younger.

The elder replied nonchalantly, "Why, from the Dragon King. He was having a picnic in the depths of this river. There was a great company assembled, with poets and storytellers and musicians to entertain them. The women who danced must have been fairies, for I have never seen such grace and beauty. Long tables were heaped with rare and tasty delicacies served on porcelain finer than eggshell. And the Dragon King! When he understood that I had come into his realm to cleanse myself of my excesses, he invited me to partake of his divine table. Never have I tasted such rich fare. This meat is so delicious that it must be dragon liver!"

Upon hearing this, the younger brother quickly threw off his clothing. "Step aside or there will be nothing left for me!" he cried, and he dove headlong into the river.

But such was his haste, that he left caution on the riverbank and hit his head on a rock at the bottom of the river. The poor man shot back to the surface with blood running red from a cut on his brow.

As the older brother hurried into the water to assist him back onto the riverbank, he said anxiously, "Little brother, what have you done to your head?"

Unable to help himself, the young storyteller replied, "It is just as you said, my brother. There was a fine feast and a great company, but the Dragon King was so insulted by my late arrival that he beat me about the head and shoulders with a drumstick!"

Needless to say, their "foolish addiction" ran far too deep ever to be washed away. But then, neither brother would have wished it otherwise.

"It's a good story that will fill your belly."
—American folk saying

The Woodcutter's Daughter

[KAZAKHSTAN]

ONCE UPON A TIME, in a smoky dugout in the barrenmost part of the steppe, there lived an aged woodcutter and his little daughter. The old woodcutter was wretchedly poor; for goods he had only a chipped ax, and for livestock, a broken-down donkey and a miserable old ox. But wise men say, "The happiness of a rich man lies in his flocks; the happiness of a poor man, in his children." And truly, the woodcutter had only to look at his daughter, and all his troubles would vanish.

His daughter was named Aina. So beautiful, so wise, and well-behaved was she, that whoever saw her fell in love on the spot. Children came riding from faraway *auls* to play with her, and grown-ups came just as far to chat with her.

One day the woodcutter loaded his bundle of wood onto his tired old donkey and bade his daughter farewell.

"Dear Aina," said he, "I am going to the bazaar and I will not be back until evening. You must not be lonely without me. If I manage to sell the firewood, I will bring you a beautiful shawl."

"May all go well with you, father," answered his daughter, "and may you have good luck! But I beg you to be careful. The bazaar, it is said, is the worst place on earth, for there fortunes are made by some and lost by others. Come back as soon as you are able. I will keep your supper warm on the fire for you."

The woodcutter gave the donkey a nudge and set forth.

When he arrived at the bazaar, he tied up the donkey to one side and began to wait for someone to buy his firewood. Time passed, but no one approached them.

At last a rich young man came wandering through the bazaar, pluming his fine black beard and preening his silken robe. He saw the ragged old man with his firewood and decided to play a trick on him.

"Say there, old man, is that firewood you are selling?" he asked.

"It is," answered the woodcutter.

"What are you asking for that bundle there?"

"One piece of silver."

"And are you selling the firewood for this price 'as-is'?"

The woodcutter did not understand the words of the young man, but seeing nothing wrong in them, he answered, "Yes."

"Very well," said the young man, "here is your silver piece. Drive your donkey after me."

When they reached the rich man's palace, the woodcutter began to untie the cord to take down the bundle of firewood. But suddenly the rich man hit him a blow on the chest and cried for everyone to hear:

"What do you think you're doing, you stupid old man? Don't tell me you want to take your donkey with you? Didn't I buy the firewood 'as-is'? That donkey belongs to me! You got your price and now you are trying to cheat me!"

The woodcutter began to object, but the young man shook his fist in the old man's face and yelled louder than ever. Then, seizing the old man by the sleeve, he dragged him off to the judge.

Wisely it is said, "A crooked rich man can make a racehorse out of an old nag, and a crooked judge, somebody else's out of what is yours," for after the judge had listened to both sides, he stroked his beard, taking in the silken robe of the rich man, and announced his verdict: The woodcutter had already received his due, and it was his own fault if he had agreed to the conditions of the buyer.

The rich man chuckled over the judge's decision and was very well pleased with his joke. But the woodcutter wept bitter tears and went grieving back to his *aul*.

While waiting, Aina had more than once to put wood on the fire to keep her father's supper warm. When at last he came stumbling wearily over the doorstep, and Aina saw the tears in his eyes, her heart went cold as ice. She threw herself into her father's arms, begging him to tell her the reason for his sadness. The woodcutter told his daughter his tale of woe, and she, with tender kisses and wise words, tried to comfort him. But only at dawn did she manage to wipe away the last of her father's tears.

Exhausted with weeping, the woodcutter was in no condition to go to work that day. Aina hugged him, saying, "Dear father! Today you are not well and you must stay in bed. Let *me* go to the bazaar. Perhaps I will be luckier than you and will sell the firewood for a better price."

At first the old man would not hear of it, but at last Aina convinced him to let her go.

"Go, my child, if you really want to," said the old man, "but know that I will have no peace until I see you again at my side."

And so Aina loaded the bundle of firewood and the chipped ax onto the old ox and set out.

At the bazaar, Aina soon saw in the crowd the young man with the fine black beard and the silken robe, strutting about, his nose in the air. When he spied the girl with the firewood, he laughed slyly to himself and went up to her.

"Hey there, little girl!" said he. "Is that firewood you're selling?"

"It is," answered Aina.

"What do you want for that bundle there?"

"Two pieces of silver."

"And will you sell the firewood for that price 'as-is'?"

"I will, but only if you give me the money 'as-is'."

"Agreed, agreed," said the rich man hastily, smiling into his beard. "Drive the ox after me."

When they came to the rich man's house, Aina said, "Now show me where to tie up the ox."

The rich man was surprised, but he pointed to a post in the middle of the courtyard. Aina tied up the ox and asked for her money. When the rich man held out two pieces of silver, she said, "But uncle, you bought my firewood 'as-is', and I gave you the ox along with the firewood. You promised to give me the money also 'as-is'. I want not only the two pieces of silver, but your open hand as well!"

The rich man was struck dumb. When he came to his senses, he began screaming and cursing, but no matter how he threatened her, Aina, ax in hand, stood firm. Finally there was nothing to do but go off together to the judge.

The judge listened but this time, though he could stroke his beard and stare at the rich man's robe all he wanted, he could not think of a way to let the rich man off. "It is my decision," he said at last, "that the buyer must give the maiden two pieces of silver for the firewood and fifty pieces of gold for his hand."

At this the rich man flew into a rage and was ready to give up the firewood, the broken-down donkey, the miserable old ox, the chipped ax, and all, but it was too late. Handing the money to Aina, he said, "You may have outsmarted me this time, wretched girl, but don't think you are going to go bragging to anybody about this. I'm still smarter than you are, and just to show you, let's make a wager. I'll tell the most fantastic thing that ever happened to me, and you do the same. Whoever's story is more fantastic, and whoever does not call the other a liar, wins. Do you agree to these conditions? I will wager the fifty gold pieces and you can wager whatever you wish."

"I agree, uncle," answered Aina. "I will wager you my own head. If you win, you can do what you will with my life. And as you are older than I in years, you must begin."

The rich man winked at the judge and began his story.

"One day I found three grains of wheat in my pocket. I threw them out the window and in no time there appeared a wheat field so tall and thick that people on camels and horses could ride about it for days. And one day, what do you think happened? Forty of my best goats strayed into the field and got lost. I called them and called them, but the goats had vanished without a trace. Fall came, the wheat ripened. My workers harvested the wheat, but the bones of the goats were nowhere to be found. They threshed the wheat, and still there was no sign of the goats. One day I asked my wife to bake me some bread, and while I was waiting I sat down to read the Koran. My wife took the bread from the fire and handed it to me. I bit off a piece and began to chew. Suddenly there was such a shrieking and bleating in my head that my mouth flew open, and out leaped forty goats, one right after the other! Before my very eyes they began capering about on the Koran. And so fat were they that each was as big as a four-year-old bull calf!"

When the rich man had finished his story, even the judge shook his head reproachfully, but Aina was unmoved.

"Uncle," said she, "I see that your story is the purest of truth. Clever men like you often have even funnier adventures. Now listen to my story." And Aina began her tale.

"One day, I planted in the middle of my *aul* a tiny cotton seed, and what do you think happened? The next day on that spot there appeared a cotton plant, which reached to the clouds, and its shadow was as long as a three-day journey. When the cotton ripened, I picked it, cleaned it, and sold it to a poor woman I know. With the money, I bought forty of the best one-humped camels, loaded them with precious cloths, and sent my eldest brother to take the caravan to Bokhara. It has been three years since my brother left and I have not yet heard one word from him. But not long ago, I heard it said that he was overtaken on the road and murdered by some blackbearded villain. I did not hope, uncle, ever to find that villain, but fate has been kind to me. I see that you are the murderer, for that is my brother's silken robe you are wearing!"

When Aina said these words, the judge fairly leaped from his seat, and the rich man fell flat on the floor. Now what was to be done? To say the girl was lying meant to give her fifty gold pieces; to say that she spoke the truth would be even worse, for then she would demand recompense for her murdered brother, and forty of the finest one-humped camels, laden with precious goods, besides.

Finally the rich man could bear it no longer.

"May your tongue stick to a stone!" he cried. "It's all lies, lies, lies, you wretched girl! Take your fifty gold pieces, take my robe too, only get out of my sight before I wring your neck!"

Aina took the gold, wrapped it in the rich man's robe and ran home to her father as fast as her legs would carry her. The woodcutter, anxious at his daughter's long absence, had come out onto the steppe to look for her. Soon he caught sight of her running toward him. He threw his arms around her neck and cried:

"Aina, my little beaver hat! What happened to you? Where have you been for such a long time, and why isn't the old ox with you?"

"May blue skies always shine upon you, father," Aina answered, "I have returned safely from the city where I sold the ox to the black-bearded rich man 'as-is'."

"My poor child," moaned the woodcutter, "the hard-hearted rich man has deceived you. Now we are lost and it is all my fault."

"Father dear," said Aina, "do not be so quick to despair. I received a very good price for the firewood and the ox."

And she held out to her father the rolled-up silken robe.

"That is a beautiful and costly robe indeed," said the woodcutter sadly, "but what good will it do me, a poor woodcutter? Without the ax, the old donkey, and the ox, we will have to live on alms."

Then Aina, saying not a word, unrolled the silken robe, and from it fell the fifty gold pieces and the two pieces of silver. The woodcutter looked in amazement, first at the glittering coins, then at his daughter, and could hardly believe it was not a dream. The girl threw her arms around his neck and told him everything that had happened in the town.

The woodcutter laughed and cried as he listened to his daughter. Aina finished her story with these words:

"O father, where the rich man is sly, the poor man is wise. The blackbeard received his just deserts, and with his fifty gold pieces we shall live happy and content to the rest of our days."

"You should have seen the fish that got away!"
—Turkish folk saying

Cutting a Story Down to Size

[UNITED STATES]

THERE WERE TWO GOOD FRIENDS who loved to while away an afternoon fishing. But they were better known for their "fish stories" than for their skill as fishermen. They had plenty of practice telling stories, for that is how they passed the time while waiting for a bite.

One day they sat on a sunny riverbank and dropped their lines into the water. One fisherman said to the other, "Did I tell you I went fishing last night? I caught a fish that was three feet long if it was an inch!"

"Really!" replied his friend. "I went fishing last night, too. I dropped my line into the water and it wasn't two minutes before I felt a tug. When I pulled in my line, there was a lantern on my hook and it was still burning!"

"Wait just a gol'darn minute there," said the first fisherman. "How could that lantern still be burning when it had been in the water?"

"I'll tell you what," said his friend. "If you cut a couple of feet off your fish, I'll blow out my lantern."

"A word to the wise is sufficient."
—English folk saying

The Most Noble Story

[MEXICO]

THERE WAS ONCE A WIDOW who had three sons, Alberto, Eduardo, and Ernesto. The old woman had spent a lifetime trying to teach her children the meaning of charity and compassion. But the day came when their mother knew that she was dying, and she would no longer be there to guide them. She called her sons to her bedside and said, "I am not a wealthy woman. The only thing of value I have to leave you is my diamond ring. It was given to me by my mother, who had it from her mother, whose mother had handed it down to her. It cannot be divided and it must not be sold, for one day it shall go to one of your daughters. Now I am faced with a most difficult task; I must decide which of you is most worthy of inheriting this treasure from me. Go out, my sons, and do good in the world. Come back to me after one week's time and tell me your stories. The one who has performed the most noble deed shall have the diamond."

By the time the week had passed, their poor mother was very near death. The three young men gathered at her bedside and she said to her firstborn, "Alberto, tell me your story."

"Well, Mother," said the eldest, "after much thought, I took careful stock of all that I owned and I gave half of everything to the poor."

"My son," said the old woman, "no one can tell you that you have not performed a good deed. But it is not a noble deed, for have I not taught you that it is everyone's responsibility to take care of the needy?"

The old woman then said to her secondborn, "Eduardo, tell me your story."

"Mama, I was passing by the river when I saw a small child being swept away in the current. As you know, I can hardly swim, but I jumped into the water and pulled the child out. I saved her from drowning and it was only by the grace of God that I didn't drown myself."

"My son, you too have done a good deed, but it is not a noble deed," said his mother. "Have I not taught you that everyone should be willing to lay his life down for that of a helpless child?"

Then the old widow called to her youngest son. "Ernesto, come tell me your story."

Ernesto hesitated, then went to his mother's bedside and took her hand. "*Mamacita*, I have not much of a story to tell. As you know, I have no earthly goods to give to the poor, and I cannot swim a stroke. But I will tell you something that happened to me this week. It was very early one morning when I was walking up in the mountains. I came upon a man sleeping at the edge of a cliff. I knew at a glance that if he were to stir in his sleep, he would fall to his death on the rocks below. I determined to prevent this tragedy. I crept over to the sleeping man as quietly as I could, so as not to startle him awake. When I got closer, I could see that it was none other than my most bitter enemy, Juan Miguel. At first, I thought to leave him there, for the last time we met, Juan had threatened to kill me if ever he got the chance. But deep down I knew what I had to do.

"As I put my arms around him, Juan awoke and I could see the fear in his eyes as he recognized me.

" 'Do not be afraid,' I told him. Then I quickly rolled him away from the precipice to safety and helped him to his feet. When Juan Miguel came toward me, at first I thought he meant to carry out his threat to kill me. But then he threw his arms around me and embraced me.

"Juan told me, 'Last night darkness fell before I could get home. Rather than chance a misstep in the dark, I decided to spend the night where I was. I had no idea that I was so close to the edge of the cliff. Surely you have saved my life, and after I treated you so poorly!'

"To make a long story short, *Mamacita*, Juan and I are no longer enemies, but have sworn to be friends forever."

The old woman shed tears of joy. "My son," she cried, "I have taught you well. That was truly a noble deed and you are a noble man, for you risked your life to save one who had sworn to kill you. With one act of kindness, you have transformed hatred into love and made the world a better place." With her dying breath she told her sons, "The diamond shall go to Ernesto, but you must all three remember that with each noble deed you perform you shall add to the treasure that awaits you in heaven."

All three sons married and had children of their own, and they, like their mother, taught their children the meaning of charity and compassion. When the time came, Ernesto left his mother's diamond to one of his daughters. But Alberto and Eduardo left their children a gem worth as much as any diamond, for their children held in their hearts their grandmother's precious legacy, the story of the most noble story.

"A liar ought to have a good memory."
—English folk saying

Ali the Persian

[IRAQ]

CALIPH HARUN AL-RASHID WAS RESTLESS and could not sleep. Whenever he felt wakeful and troubled, he sent for the storyteller known as Ali the Persian. Ali the Persian could lift all burdens from the heaviest of hearts with his amusing tales. That night, when the storyteller appeared before the caliph, he bowed and said, "I am at your command, O Great One."

"Ali, my heart is heavy tonight and I would have one of the jewels from your treasure store of tales to brighten my melancholy."

"To hear is to obey," replied the storyteller. "But let me first ask you, my lord, would you have me tell a story that I have seen with my own eyes or one that I have heard with my own ears?"

"I know that you have traveled far and wide. I do not doubt, Ali, that you have seen much that merits telling."

"Then I shall tell you a true story and one that I have seen with my own eyes. Know, Your Magnificence, that some years ago I left my beloved Baghdad on a journey. With me I brought a leather bag in which I carried a few belongings. No sooner had I made my way to the marketplace of a nearby city, when a rascally fellow seized my leather bag and shouted, 'This is *my* bag!'

"You can imagine my dismay, my lord," continued Ali. "Of course I decried him a liar to the gathering crowd. It was not long before we were ushered into the presence of the Kazi, the district magistrate, to have our dispute settled."

" 'State your cases,' said the Kazi. 'Which one of you is the plaintiff?'

"Even as I stepped forward, so did that false fellow. That shameless thief pointed at my bag and cried, 'Truly, Your Honor, that is my bag. Only yesterday I lost it, and I could not believe my good fortune when today I saw this rogue in the market making so free with it.' "

Ali the Persian told the caliph, "I sputtered with outrage at that rascal's bold lies and said to the Kazi, 'Your Honor, he lies like a jackal! I have only just arrived in your city. How could I have taken the bag when yesterday I was in my own city of Baghdad?'

"The Kazi looked from one of us to the other. Then he turned to the thief and said, 'If this is truly your bag, you will know what is inside. Describe the contents.'

"Bold as brass, the rascal looked the Kazi in the eye and said, 'That is easy to do, Your Honor. In my bag I had a kerchief and two candlesticks. There were also two platters, two spoons, and a cushion. Moreover, my bag contained two leather rugs and a brass tray and two basins and a cooking pot and two water jars and a ladle. In addition, there was a cow and two calves and a she-goat and two kids and a ewe and two lambs and a lioness and two lions and a she-bear and two jackals and the finest camel in the village. And, of course, I carried in my bag two tents, a mattress and two sofas to go with them, two sitting rooms, a kitchen with two doors, and a company of Kurds who will bear witness that this is my bag!'

"The Kazi frowned at his testimony and said to me, 'And what do *you* say was in the bag, Ali?'

"So I stepped forward and said, 'Truthfully, Your Honor, there was nothing in my bag but a loaf of bread, a chunk of cheese, a lemon, a few olives . . . and . . . ,' (I glared at the market thief, hoping that perhaps I could kill him with a look), '. . . a ruined little tenement. And did I mention the other tenement, the one without the door?

And the dog house and the boys' school and several young men playing dice. In addition, my bag contained the cities of Bassorah and Baghdad. You see, I miss my native city so much when I travel abroad that I have taken to bringing it along with me. In that bag I also kept a palace, an ironsmith's forge, a fishing net, and a thousand merchants who will be glad to testify that this is my bag!'

"At my testimony, the lying market thief began to weep. He wailed, 'My lord Kazi, who doesn't know that in my bag I carry castles and citadels and men playing chess? Furthermore, in my bag I have a brood-mare, two colts, and a stallion. It also contains a blind man and two lamenters, a Christian ecclesiastic, two deacons, two monks, a Kazi and two assessors, who will be more than happy to give evidence that this is my bag!'

"By now, my lord," said the storyteller to the caliph, "the Kazi's ears were as red as a Persian rose when he turned to me and said, " 'Ali, what do you have to say to this?'

"So I replied respectfully, 'Allah keep our lord the Kazi! I had in this leather bag a coat of mail and a broadsword and several armories. I also had a thousand fighting rams, a thousand barking dogs, and a sheepfold with its pasturage. In addition, it held gardens and vines and flowers, figs and apples and statues, pictures and flagons and goblets, singing women and marriage feasts and brothers of success, which I must confess were robbers. There was also a small company of daybreak-raiders, five Abyssinian women, three Hindi maidens, and a score of Greek girls. It also contained the Tigris and the Euphrates, a thousand stables, mosques, and baths, twenty storehouses full of victuals, one plank and one nail, Gaza, Askalon, and the kingdom of Solomon. And last but not least (may Allah preserve our Kazi), a thousand sharp razors to shave off the Kazi's beard, unless he adjudges this bag to be mine!'

"You may be sure," confided Ali the Persian, "that the Kazi's face turned as purple as Tyrian silk when he roared, 'I can see that you are both pestilent rogues who make sport of poor magistrates who are simply trying to uphold the law. Never did tongue tell nor ear hear more insolent lies than mine have heard today! Is this leather bag a bottomless sea?'

"The outraged Kazi then seized the bag, threw it at me, and commanded, 'Open this bag, Ali, and show us the contents of this miraculous vessel!'

"So I opened the bag, and behold! There was nothing but a loaf of bread, a chunk of cheese, a lemon, and a few olives! So disgusted was I at the mundane contents of the bag that I threw it down before the market thief and went straightaway home to Baghdad!"

When the caliph heard this, he laughed until the tears came to his eyes. And when Ali the Persian went home that night, he carried more than bread and cheese in his bag, for the caliph was a wise man and knew the worth of a good story.

"Some lies are better than the truth."
—Turkish folk saying

The Four Ne'er-do-wells

[AFGHANISTAN (JEWISH)]

FOUR NE'ER-DO-WELLS found themselves down on their luck. They had no money, no food, and no prospects. Along the road, they passed a rich man's house. Outside the house was a garden and in that garden there was an abundance of ripe fruit. Just to look at the twining grape vines and the luscious apricot, pear, and apple trees made their bellies growl with hunger. The four starving men crept over the stone wall and began to fill their pockets and their mouths with fruit. But in their haste, they forgot all caution.

"What are you doing here?" came a loud roar. The four ne'er-do-wells looked up to see the angry owner of the garden; they had been caught red-handed.

"Who are you and what are you doing in my garden?" shouted the rich man, shaking his fist.

"Hee-haw!" brayed the first thief. "Can't you see I'm a donkey? I'm just a poor dumb beast; I had no way of knowing it was your garden."

"Humph!" snorted the rich man. "And what about you?" he asked the second thief, who had been so startled by the owner's appearance that he had fallen to the ground. "I suppose you are a donkey too?"

"Oh, no!" said the thief, who began to flip and flop about on the ground where he lay. "Can't you see that I am a fish? There was a terrible storm. One minute I was happily swimming about the ocean with all my brothers and sisters, and the next minute I found myself washed ashore in the company of a donkey! The sea squall has blown over, but now I am stranded!"

"Harumph!" scoffed the rich man. Turning to the third ne'er-do-well, he scowled, "You had better have a better explanation for being here in my garden!"

"Well, I am just an innocent sailor," he replied. "I was standing on the deck of my ship, when the same squall that blew that fish out of the water blew me here as well."

"Then how come you are holding a fistful of my grapes, sailor?" demanded the rich man.

"You know," shrugged the thief, "I was just asking myself the same question."

The rich man shook his head at the audacity of the man and turned to confront the fourth thief, who still clung to the top branches of the apricot tree he had been raiding. "You up there," growled the rich man. "I suppose you have some wild story to tell?"

"Not at all," said the last of the four ne'er-do-wells. "I'm just a nightingale stopping to light on my way home."

"Ha!" trumpeted the rich man. "If you are a nightingale, then sing me a song and prove it."

Unfortunately, the last thief was tone deaf and could not have carried a tune if his life—or his freedom—depended upon it. He squeaked out such sour notes that even his companions had to cover their ears.

The rich man shouted, "Enough! Do you call that a song? It sounds more like the tortured bray of a dying donkey!"

"Well, between you and me," confided the thief, "your apricots are nothing to brag about either!"

The corners of the rich man's mouth trembled as he tried to stifle his laughter, but at last a smile broke free and turned into a belly laugh that shook his sides. "Never in my life have I heard such a pack of lies . . . but they are clever ones at that. Fill your pockets and your bellies, you rogues, and be on your way. But if I ever catch you stealing from my garden again, donkey, I shall harness you up and put you to work in my field. Fish, I shall throw you back into the sea. And I shall force you, sailor, to listen to the sour notes of that tone-deaf nightingale for the rest of your days."

The four grateful men thanked the rich man and hurried along their way. As for the rich man, he was amply repaid for his generosity, for now he, too, had a good story to tell.

"A good tale is not the worse for being told twice."
—American folk saying

The Story Spirits

[KOREA]

LONG AGO IN THE LAND OF KOREA, there was a young boy, the only child born to a rich mother and father. Above all things, the little boy loved to hear stories. Whenever he was introduced to a new person, he would beg, "Tell me a story—one I haven't heard before."

In that household there was an old servant who knew a great many stories, and he soon became a favorite of the young boy. At bedtime each night the old man would tell him stories of fox spirits and dragons, clever princesses and wicked tigers. The boy kept those stories in a leather bag that hung from a nail on his wall. Each new story the boy heard went into that bag, which was tied shut with a string so that it might not escape.

Sometimes the boy would boast to his friends about the wonderful stories that the old servant told him each night. His friends would plead for a story. But the selfish boy always refused to share even a short one. "They are *my* stories," he would say. "Go find your own."

So the years went by. Each new story the boy heard was jammed and crammed into that old leather bag until it grew quite crowded and close and uncomfortable, for never was a story allowed to go free.

The story-loving boy grew into a young man and still he hoarded his stories. At first the stories were merely discontent, but as year after year went by, the story spirits grew more and more angry.

The young man's parents died, but the faithful old storyteller stayed by his side and cared for him. When the young man came of an age to be married, his uncle was able to arrange a marriage with a wealthy bride from a good family.

On the day before the the wedding, the old servant was shuffling past the young man's room when he heard faint whispers from within. "That's odd," said the servant to himself. "I thought my master was out today." There was something about the bitter tone of the voices that worried the old man. He stopped at the doorway and listened.

"So he's going to be married?" came a gruff voice from somewhere in that room.

"He'll be free to enjoy himself," whispered another angry voice, "while we must remain prisoners in the dark."

It was with shock and horror that the servant realized that the voices were coming from the story bag! The old storyteller knew at once that they must belong to story spirits. He listened on.

"It is time we had our revenge," grumbled one of the spirits.

"Yes, yes," came a jumble of voices. "But how?"

"It is a long ride to the bride's home, where the wedding will take place," said one. "He will surely grow thirsty. I shall turn into a well filled with cool spring water. He will never suspect that I am poisoned."

"If for some reason he does not drink from the well," said a second story spirit, "I will change myself into a patch of bright red strawberries. But when he plucks a berry and eats it, he will die."

"And if that does not work," added a third, "I will take over. When they place the bag of chaff beneath his horse so that he may dismount, I will be a red-hot poker hidden inside the bag. When he steps on me, I will burn his feet so badly that they will have to call off the wedding."

"And if your plan fails," laughed another story spirit bitterly, "I shall wait for the bride and groom in their bed chamber. When everyone is asleep, I shall turn into a poisonous snake and bite them."

The servant tiptoed away, wringing his hands. "What shall I do?" he wondered frantically. "If I tell the boy's uncle, he will call me an old fool and forbid me to speak to my master. And even if I were to warn my master, he would not believe me." The old servant stayed up half the night working out a plan.

In the morning, as the household prepared for the journey to the bride's home, the old servant begged to be allowed to lead his master's horse.

"You are too old for such a long journey," replied the bridegroom. But the old man insisted and, as he was a favorite of his master, at last it was permitted. The sun rose high as the wedding procession made its way. When they passed a well at the side of the road, the young man told his servant, "Stop here and I shall drink."

To the surprise of the bridegroom and the outrage of his uncle, the servant walked right past the well saying, "You shall have a cool drink of water when we arrive at your bride's house."

Then they passed a fragrant field of bright red strawberries. "One of those berries will quench my thirst," said the young man. "Stop the horse and pick me one," he ordered. But the old man cracked his whip and urged the horse on even faster, pretending not to hear.

The bridegroom's uncle said to his nephew, "Such insolence in a servant is unheard of. He must be properly disciplined."

"I don't understand," replied the young man. "He has never acted this way before. Perhaps he is overly eager to see me wed. Could we not wait until after the wedding to punish him?"

"Very well," agreed his uncle. "But as soon as we return home, he will be dealt with harshly."

When at last they arrived at the bride's home, they were greeted by crowds of well-wishers. A bag of chaff was brought over for the groom to step down onto when he dismounted from his horse. But the old servant pretended to stumble and he pushed his master to one side. The bridegroom fell to the ground, much to the embarrassment of everyone present. Again the uncle fumed. But the old man was too concerned for the safety of his charge to heed his angry look. All through the wedding and the feast that followed, the faithful servant kept a watchful eye over his master, in case the story spirits should seek their revenge in some unexpected manner.

At last the guests went home and the newlywed couple retired to their bed chamber. No sooner had the light been extinguished, when there was a loud pounding on their door. In burst the servant brandishing a sword. His master was now convinced that the old man had truly lost his mind.

"Get out of bed, master!" shouted the servant.

"What is the meaning of this?" replied the young man angrily.

"There is no time to answer questions! Do as I tell you at once!"

No sooner had the groom and bride leapt up from their bed then the old man threw back the mat they slept on. Coiled beneath it was a huge poisonous snake, ready to strike. The servant fell upon the snake with his sword and killed it.

The bride's parents and the young man's uncle heard the commotion and came crowding into the room. Only then did the old servant dare explain his peculiar behavior. They then understood that he had saved the young couple's lives. The uncle begged his forgiveness and the servant was rewarded generously for his loyalty and courage.

"I see that I am to blame for all this," said the young man. "Never again shall I refuse a story to anyone who asks." And he was true to his word. No longer did he hoard the stories in his story bag. He began by telling them to his bride and, after they were blessed with children, he regaled his sons and daughters with his stories. In time, he came to be known as one of the finest storytellers in all of Korea. As for the story spirits, they were thus appeased and never again threatened the young man. Told and re-told, many people have shared his stories, including this one.

"One story brings on another."
—Irish folk saying

The Humbled Storyteller

[RUSSIA]

THERE WAS ONCE A STORYTELLER who had spent many years wandering throughout Russia, telling tales for his bread. This storyteller was skilled in his art and, as the years passed, he became known far and wide for his tall tales. The day came when the storyteller no longer had to take to the roads in search of an audience, for his audiences had begun to seek him out. He settled down in the city of Tashkent. When merchants and pilgrims came to the bustling city, they were certain to visit the storyteller and hear him tell his tales before returning to their homes. And whenever the storyteller entertained an audience, he was well rewarded. His reputation grew as tall as his tales and he became very well-to-do. He lived in a big house with servants to wait upon him. He dined on only the finest fare, wore robes of silk and velvet, and had a ring for every finger. But the storyteller's good fortune went to his head, and he grew very vain.

One story leads to another and, when travelers came to hear the storyteller's tales, they also brought stories of their own. One night, after being entertained at the storyteller's house, a visitor told him, "Indeed you are a master of the tall tale . . ."

The storyteller, accustomed to praise, smiled smugly at the compliment.

". . . but," the stranger added, "should you ever journey down to the shores of the Aral Sea, you must come to my village and listen to our storyteller. He has tales the like of which you have never heard before!"

As the visitor took his leave, the storyteller said to himself, "Stories the like of which I have never heard before! I am the greatest storyteller in all the land. Everyone says so; it must be true!"

And yet, the seed of doubt had been planted in his mind. Could a village bumpkin truly tell stories as well as he, the famed storyteller of Tashkent? He could no longer sleep at night, but lay in his bed wondering, worrying whether the visitor had spoken the truth. The storyteller's temper grew as short as his tales were tall.

"I must settle this question once and for all!" he cried. That very day, the storyteller closed up his house, bought a camel, and joined a caravan of merchants traveling across the desert. When that long and difficult leg of his journey was completed, he booked passage on a ship and sailed down the Syr Darya to the Aral Sea.

At the very edge of the sea was the little village in which the storyteller's rival made his home. The famed teller of Tashkent asked for the whereabouts of the village teller and was directed to a humble little dwelling in the heart of the village. "This fellow can't be much of a storyteller if he cannot afford a better house than this," scoffed the man of Tashkent.

Puffing up his chest, the storyteller wasted no time, but strode up to the door and knocked. The door swung open and before him stood a small girl.

"I wish to speak to your father," said the storyteller.

"My father is taking a nap," replied the little girl.

The storyteller thought to have some fun with the child. He said, "Would you be so good as to tell your father that I have come all the way from Tashkent to hear his stories? Tell him that I have brought him the gift of a rug. By the time my servants have finished unrolling it, the rug will stretch all the way from the dock to your father's house."

The little girl's eyes sparkled, but she nodded solemnly and replied, "Your visit is very timely then. Only yesterday a spark from my grandmother's pipe burned a little hole in our rug and your rug will be just the right size to patch it."

The storyteller grew pale. If this small child could tell such an outrageous lie without blinking an eye, he knew that he could never come up with a story to best her father.

Without another word, he turned on his heels and returned to the ship. The proud storyteller went home a wiser and humbler man.

"Tell a story, compose a lie, or get out."
—Irish folk saying

The Storyteller at Fault

[IRELAND]

LONG AGO THERE REIGNED IN LEINSTER a king who was very fond of stories. Like the other princes and chieftains of Erin, he had a favorite storyteller. The king had given his storyteller hounds, horses, and a fine estate. All he asked in return was a new story each night before he went to sleep. Such was the skill of the storyteller that he had never failed to help the king forget his worries and lose himself in the wonder of his stories. And so numerous were the stories in the storyteller's head that he had grown old in the service of his king and yet had never told the same story twice.

One morning the storyteller rose early, as was his custom, and strolled in the garden to think of a new story for the king. But he found himself quite at fault, unable to think of anything new or strange to tell about. He could get no further than "There was once a king who had three sons . . ." or "One day the king of all Ireland . . ." before his wife was calling him in to breakfast.

"I cannot eat," replied the storyteller. "As long as I have been in the service of the king of Leinster, I have never sat down to breakfast without having a new story ready for the evening. But today, my mind refuses to work for me; tonight I shall be disgraced forever when the king calls for his storyteller."

Just then his wife looked up and said, "What is that thing at the end of the field?"

The storyteller whistled for his favorite hound and they walked over to see for themselves. They found a tattered old beggarman with a wooden leg, who was shaking some dice in a cup.

"Who are you, my good man?" asked the storyteller.

"Just a poor, old, lame, decrepit, miserable creature," replied the old man. "I'm waiting here to see if anyone will play a game of dice with me."

"Play with you!" exclaimed the storyteller. "What has a beggar like you to play for?"

"I have one hundred pieces of gold in my purse. That is worth a roll of the dice, is it not?"

"Go on," whispered the storyteller's wife. "Play with him and perhaps you will have something to tell the king tonight."

So the storyteller agreed. A smooth stone was set between the two men, and upon that stone they cast their throws. Before the storyteller knew what had happened, he had lost every penny he possessed to the old beggar.

"Will you play again?" asked the old man.

"You have all my money," frowned the storyteller.

"Haven't you horses, hounds, and carriage? Perhaps you'd win," winked the old man.

"Perhaps I wouldn't," replied the storyteller. "I'll not have my wife tramping about on foot."

But his wife urged him on. "Go on, love. I don't mind walking, if you don't."

Reluctantly the storyteller rolled the dice again, and in one throw he lost hounds, horse, and carriage.

"Will you play again?" asked the beggar.

"Are you making fun of me? What have I left to stake?" grumbled the storyteller.

The ragged old man smiled slyly and said, "I'd stake all my winnings against your wife."

The storyteller glared at him and turned to leave. But his wife drew him back and said, "Accept his offer, love. The third time is always the lucky one. Surely this time you will win."

"I've never refused you before, but you can't mean what you're saying?"

"Go on," she urged. "Go on."

With a sigh, the storyteller picked up the cup and rolled again, but with no better luck than he'd had before. Without a word, his wife went and sat down beside the old beggarman.

"You're in that much of a hurry to leave me?" asked the storyteller angrily.

His wife shrugged and said, "Sure I was won fair and square. You wouldn't want me to cheat the poor man, would you?"

The beggarman chuckled and patted her hand. Then he said to her husband, "I'll stake the whole lot now, wife and all, against your own self."

"And welcome to it," said the miserable storyteller. "I've nothing left to lose."

Again they played and again the storyteller lost. "Well, here I am," he groaned. "What do you want with me?"

"You'll see soon enough," said the old man. "But for now, would you rather be a deer, a fox, or a hare?"

"A hare is as good as anything," said the storyteller.

The beggar struck the storyteller with a wand. Suddenly the poor fellow was a hare skipping about on the green. Before he could twitch his ears, who but his own dear wife set his favorite hound after him! Up and down the furrows, in and out of the bushes he ran, with the dog nipping and snapping at his heels. Once he tried to hide behind his wife's skirts, but she kicked him away. Finally the beggar reached down and snatched up the exhausted hare by the scruff of the neck. He struck him with his wand, and once again the storyteller stood before them, panting and breathless.

Wide-eyed with terror, the storyteller cried, "Why would you take such pleasure in plaguing a poor man like me?"

"I suppose it's because I'm an odd kind of good-for-nothing fellow," replied the old man. "But come with me now and you'll have a better answer to your question." The beggarman tapped the storyteller with his wand and the poor man found himself standing in the great hall of Red Hugh O'Donnell's castle. It was soon obvious to the storyteller that he was invisible to those around him. Hardly a minute went by before O'Donnell's doorkeeper entered the hall, and who should be with him but the very same tattered old beggarman.

"Greetings, O'Donnell," said the beggar. "Are you of a mind to be entertained? Five pieces of silver and I'll show you a trick to open your eyes."

"That you shall have," said O'Donnell.

So the tattered old man took out three small straws and laid them out on the table. "The middle straw I shall blow away and leave the other two where they are."

"You can't blow away one without blowing them all away," said O'Donnell.

The beggarman winked and said, "Can't I now?" With that, he placed a finger on the two outside straws, gave a good puff, and blew away the middle one.

"That's a good trick," laughed O'Donnell, and he gave him five pieces of silver.

"Hah!" said one of O'Donnell's sons. "You call that a trick! For half the money I'll do the same." The lad laid out the three straws in a row, placed a finger on each of the outside straws, and blew. But to the astonishment of all present, when the lad blew, away flew all three of the straws and his right hand with them!

"Six more pieces, O'Donnell," offered the beggarman, "and I'll do another trick for you."

"Six you shall have," promised his host.

"Watch my ears. I shall move one, but not the other."

"Your ears are big enough to look at, but however big they may be, no one can move one ear without moving the other too," said O'Donnell.

The beggarman winked slyly and said, "Can't I now?" With that, he reached up with his hand and gave a tug to one ear.

O'Donnell laughed again and paid him the six pieces.

"You call that a trick!" scoffed the handless lad. "Anyone can do that." So saying, O'Donnell's son put his remaining hand up to his ear and gave it a pull. But when he tugged, off came his ear!

"Well, O'Donnell, it's strange tricks I've shown you," said the old man, "but I'll show you a stranger one yet for the same money."

"You have my word on it," said O'Donnell.

The beggarman took a ball of silk from out of his bag and, holding onto the end of the thread, he flung the ball high into the air. To everyone's surprise, the ball disppeared from sight. The beggar reached into his bag again, drew out a long-eared hare, set it on the silken thread, and the hare scampered on up the thread and disappeared. Then the old man took O'Donnell's best hound, lifted it onto the thread, and sent it up after the hare. It too went running up the silken thread until it disappeared from sight.

"Now," said the beggar to the gathered crowd, "has anyone a mind to run after the dog?"

"I will," said the handless earless lad of O'Donnell's.

"Up with you then," said the old man, "but if you let any harm come to the hare, I'll have your head."

The lad scoffed and ran up the thread after the other two, until all three were lost from sight. After a time, the beggarman announced, "That lad has fallen asleep and has let the hound eat the hare." He began to wind up the silken thread. Down came the sleeping lad and the hound, still licking his chops, but no hare.

"I warned you that I'd have your head if any harm came to my hare," said the old man to the lad. He took up a sword and struck off the head of both boy and hound.

"Now, you've gone too far," roared O'Donnell.

"Five pieces of silver for each of them," replied the beggar, "and they shall have their heads back."

"Done," said O'Donnell.

With a wave of the beggarman's hand, the hound's head and lad's head, hand, and ear jumped back to where they belonged. "Now I'll give *you* five pieces of silver," laughed the old man, "if ever again that hound touches a hare or that lad makes a foolish boast!"

Suddenly the invisible storyteller, who had been watching the strange scene in amazement, felt himself hurtling through the air. In terror, the poor man closed his eyes. When he opened them again, he found himself standing behind the throne of his own master, the king of Leinster. Though the storyteller could see the king and his courtiers, it was obvious that he was invisible to them.

"I'm ready for my story," called the king to his doorkeeper. "Fetch me my storyteller."

The doorkeeper ran off to do his king's bidding. In only a short while he returned, followed by the same old ragged beggarman, his toes peeping through his shoes and his ears poking out of his hat. Only now the old man held a harp in his hand.

"Your Majesty," said the doorkeeper, "the storyteller was nowhere to be found, but this fellow says he can play the harp for you."

"It is the storyteller I want and no harper, for I already have the best harpers in all of Erin," boasted the king to the old beggar. The king then signalled to his harpers to play. When they were finished, the king said to the old man, "Have you ever heard the like?"

"I have indeed, Your Majesty," replied the old man, "every time I hear the buzz of the beetles at twilight or the screech of a wet, angry cat."

When the king's harpers heard that, they were so outraged that they drew their swords and attacked the old man. But instead of striking the beggar down, their blows fell upon each other.

"Hang that rogue!" cried the king. "If I can't have my story, then at least let me have my peace!"

The guards seized the old beggar, marched him up to the gallows, and hanged him. But when they returned to the great hall, who should they see but the old beggarman seated on a bench. He winked and raised a flagon of ale to them in greeting.

"Didn't we just hang you?" asked the captain of the guards. He ran back to the scaffold and who should he find hanging by the neck but the king's favorite brother!

Reluctantly, the captain returned to the hall. "Your Majesty, we just hanged that vagabond, but here he is alive and well again," he reported, though he thought it prudent not to make mention of the king's brother.

"Hang him again," roared the king.

They did as they were told, but this time they found the king's chief harper hanging where the tattered beggarman should have been. When they returned to the hall, the old beggarman chuckled, "Would you be hanging me a third time now?"

" 'Tis trouble enough you've caused," said the king to the little beggarman. "I'll not try to hang you again, if only you'll take yourself as far away from here as your feet will carry you."

"Ah, now, that's a more reasonable fellow!" laughed the old man. "And since you've given up trying to hang a stranger because he finds fault with your music, I don't mind telling you that you'll find your friends sitting in the shade of the gallows enjoying a flagon of ale!"

As soon as the old man spoke those words, the invisible storyteller again found himself hurtling through the air. When he opened his eyes, he was astonished to find himself back in the field by his house in the company of his wife and the ragged old beggarman.

The beggar slapped the dazed storyteller on the back and laughed heartily. "I'll torment you no more, poor fellow. There's your wife and your horse, your money and your house all back again to do with as you please."

"I thank you for my horse and my hound," frowned the storyteller, "but my money and my wife you may keep. Who ever thought that my own wife would cast me aside for a ragged old beggar?"

"Don't think ill of your wife, my friend," replied the old man. "Forgive and forget, as husband and wife should do. She couldn't help herself, for the same power that changed your body bewitched her mind. Have you ever heard of Angus of the Bruff?"

"Who has not heard of the greatest magician in all of Erin?" replied the storyteller.

"Well, I am no other than Angus himself. This morning my magic told me of your trouble and I came to your aid. Now when the king of Leinster calls for you tonight, you have quite a story to tell him!" With one last wave of the hand, he disappeared, leaving the storyteller and his wife shaking their heads in wonder.

It was true enough that the storyteller now had a story fit for a king. From first to last, he told the king of Leinster all that had befallen him. The king laughed so long and so hard that he couldn't go to sleep at all that night. But best of all, he told the storyteller never to trouble himself for a fresh story. Every night, for as long as he lived, the king of Leinster listened again and laughed afresh at the tale of the tattered beggarman and the storyteller at fault.

II

ONE FOR THE LISTENER

"If you're going to tell a lie, tell it big enough
so that no one will believe you."
—American folk saying

Now, That's a Story!

[HUNGARY]

THERE WAS ONCE A PRINCESS who loved to listen to stories. When the people in her father's court had told her all the stories they knew, the king summoned storytellers from throughout the land to entertain his daughter. But the more tales the princess heard, the fewer there remained that she had not heard. She even decided that when she married, it would be only to someone who could serve her up a story she had never heard before. "That would be the man to grow old with," she told the king, "for I would never be bored."

So the princess announced that she would marry only the fellow who could get her to say "Now, that's a story!" Many came to win the hand of the princess, but she had heard too many tall tales to be easily impressed.

"I have already heard about the bull so large that if two men sat on its horns they could neither see nor hear each other. And if someone tells me one more time about the pipe so big he can light it on the sun I shall scream," cried the princess. "I want a fresh story, for I'm bored, bored, bored!"

Princes, knights, and rich merchants came to see if they might win the princess. But as soon as anyone would begin to tell her a tale, the princess would wave them away, saying, "I have heard it all before!"

Now one day a poor young peasant came knocking on their gate and requested an audience with the princess. The king took one look at the ragged fellow and could guess what he had come for, as by that time many noblemen had come on the same errand, only to be turned out by the princess.

"How dare such a ragamuffin presume to seek the hand of my daughter!" roared the king.

But he was a comely lad and the princess said to her father, "It will do no harm to listen and I am always ready to hear a good story. Besides, it is only if I say 'Now that's a story' that I shall have to marry him."

So the young peasant was admitted to the royal presence. He bowed before the king and the princess.

"Good morning, Your Majesties," said the lad.

"Good morning, my boy," replied the king. "What have you come for?"

"I have come for a wife, if you please."

"A wife!" laughed the king. "That is all well and good, but what would a man like you keep her on?"

"I dare say I could manage to keep her pretty comfortably, Your Majesty," said the lad, with a twinkle in his eye. "You see, my father has a pig."

"A pig!" scowled the king.

But the princess winked at her father, then said to the young peasant, "It must be a marvelous pig."

"It is a wonderful pig, Princess; he has kept my father, my mother, my seven sisters, and myself for the last twenty years."

"Oh?" said the princess.

"He gives us a quart of milk every morning."

"Indeed!" she remarked.

"Yes, Your Highness, and he lays the most delicious eggs for our breakfast."

"Indeed!"

"And every day my mother cuts a nice bit of bacon out of his side and by the next morning it has grown back again."

"Indeed!"

"The other day my pig disappeared. My poor mother looked high and low for him, but he was nowhere to be seen."

"That is a pity," said the princess.

"Finally she found him in the larder, catching mice."

"A very useful pig," observed the princess.

"Oh, to be sure! Why, my father sends him into town every day to run errands for him."

"That is very practical of your father," said the princess, "as long as the pig doesn't object."

"Just last week he sent the pig into town to order a new suit of clothes for me, and my father too, from Your Highness's own tailor."

"They do appear very well made," said the princess to the ragged peasant lad.

"Yes, Your Highness, and he pays all our bills with the gold he picks up from the road."

"A very precious pig," said the princess.

"But lately, he has seemed a bit unruly, and rather out of sorts."

"I am sorry to hear it."

"He refuses to do what he is told and will no longer allow my mother to take bacon from his side."

"The naughty thing," clucked the princess.

"Besides which, Your Highness, he is growing rather blind and can no longer see where he is going."

"Then shouldn't he be led?" suggested the princess.

"Yes, Princess," replied the peasant lad. "That is why my father has just hired your father to look after him."

The princess burst into laughter and exclaimed, "Now, that's a story!"

"My dear!" said the king in dismay. "Do you know what you have just done?"

"Indeed!" said his daughter.

"Perhaps we can buy the lad off and send him on his way with a bag of gold," suggested the king.

"No, Father," she replied with a smile. "I think I'll keep this one."

And so the princess and the clever young man were married. The princess never regretted her decision. Just as she had suspected, the ragged peasant lad cleaned up quite nicely, and neither she nor their children were ever bored.

*"You can't tell how far a toad will jump
by the length of his tale."*
—American folk saying

Little Bobtail

[INUIT (NATIVE AMERICAN)]

WINTER WAS COMING AND THE MICE HAD MUCH TO DO. Every day they would scurry about collecting stores of nuts and roots and berries that would have to last them through the long, cold winter. But if they worked hard each day to gather foodstores, each night they gathered a bit of summer sun and mouse magic to store in their hearts and warm them from the inside out until the spring thaw. How did they do this? Each evening, when their work was finished, they met by moonlight in a grassy little clearing for good company, a good meal, and some good stories. As they nibbled on roots and seeds, they would entertain each other with tales of foolish foxes and clever mice.

"On my way here tonight," said one little brown mouse, "I was chased by an enormous owl. If I had not ducked down into a hare's burrow, I would have been his supper by now!" All the little mouse children listened wide-eyed. The brown mouse puffed up his chest and said, "Each of the owl's claws was as big as I am and his fierce yellow eyes glowed like two full moons. On your way home tonight, stay close to your mamas, little ones, or he might just make a meal of you!" All the little mice shivered with delight and snuggled up against their mothers.

Now it so happened that among this company of mice there was a scrawny little mouse named Bobtail. The reason she was called this was because she had only a short little stump of a tail; the rest of it had been lost to a fox when she was quite young. If ever a mouse told a story at a gathering, they could be sure that Bobtail would have one to match it.

"Tell us a story, Bobtail!" cried the mice.

"Make it a scary one!" said one.

"Make it a true story!" said another.

"Tell us again how you lost your tail," begged a third little mouse.

"I won't bore you with that old story," scoffed Bobtail. "Foxes eat mice and that is the way of the world. I'm going to tell you about the time I myself made a meal of a fox!"

All the little mice gasped, "No! You didn't! A real fox?"

"Oh, yes," said Bobtail, proudly drawing herself up to her full tiny height, "and although I couldn't swear to it, I'd say it was the very fox that bit off my tail. I had been looking out for that fox for years, when I came upon him stretched out in a clearing. I'll tell you this; I was mad! Quietly I crept up to him . . ."

"Yes! Yes!" said the little mice. "What did you do then?"

"Chomp-chomp!" said Bobtail, "I chewed off one of his front legs!"

"Swear it is so!" cried the little mice.

"It is so!" said Bobtail.

"Then what?" asked the mice impatiently.

"Chomp-chomp! I chewed off the other front leg, of course!"

"Then what?"

"Chomp-chomp! I chewed off a hind leg."

"Then what?"

"Chomp-chomp! I chewed off the other one!"

"Are you *sure* this is a true story, Bobtail?" asked the brown mouse doubtfully. "Weren't you afraid to eat a fox feet first? Even a wolf will start eating his prey at the head."

"That is true," said Bobtail, "but I told you I was mad. And besides, when I found this fox, he had no head."

"No head?" asked the little mice. "How could that be?"

"Well, he was already dead when I got to him," explained Little Bobtail, "and a lucky thing for him, too!"

If Bobtail had no tail to speak of, her story-tales more than made up for that. For all through the long winter, when the icy winds howled and the snows fell, the mice kept themselves warm by telling over and over again the tale of brave little Bobtail, the mouse that ate the fox.

"God created Man because he loves stories."
—Elie Wiesel

A Fair Price for a Story

[FIJI ISLANDS (MELANESIA)]

LONG, LONG AGO ON THE ISLAND OF BEQA, the people would gather together to hear their favorite storytellers recite tales. It happened one night that Dredre, one of the greatest storytellers on all the islands, had come to tell stories to a great assembly of people there. As was the custom, the storyteller called out, "What shall your gift to Dredre be, those of you who wish to hear his story?"

Each listener in turn pledged a gift to the storyteller. It came time for a chief named Tui Qalita to name his gift. Tui Qalita wanted to give a gift that would adequately express his appreciation to Dredre, so he replied, "I promise to bring an eel in exchange for your story." Everyone present was impressed with his pledge, for eel was a delicacy eaten only by chiefs.

"Tonight my stories shall be in your honor, my chief," said Dredre to Tui Qalita. Dredre enchanted his listeners with his stories of creation, stories of the gods, and hero tales. The stories went on long into the night until, one by one, the listeners dropped off to sleep. All except Tui Qalita. He was restless and could not sleep. He was already wondering where he would find the eel he had promised as payment for Dredre's stories. If he failed to find one, he would be dishonored. The sun had barely risen when the chief set out in search of an eel.

To hunt for eel was not an easy task. They were found only by digging deep into the ground. Tui Qalita tried many places, but found no sign of an eel for the storyteller. Then he recalled having seen the hole of an eel at Namoliwai. Tui Qalita went to Namoliwai at once. He found the eel's hole and began to dig with a stick. He dug and dug until great mounds of dirt were piled high all around him. Tui Qalita thrust his hand down into the opening and he felt something move. Quickly the chief grasped at it and pulled with all his strength. He gave a great tug, then fell backwards, his hand still clutching a wriggling eel. Never had Tui Qalita seen such a big one, and it took all his strength to subdue it. At last the eel stopped struggling and the chief threw the creature over his shoulder. But then he heard a strange voice, which pleaded, "Spare my life."

With a start Tui Qalita realized that it was the eel speaking. Before his very eyes, the eel took the shape of a man. Still, Tui Qalita held fast to the eel man' s arm. "I promised the storyteller an eel," said Tui Qalita. "You must go back with me, for I have nothing else to offer."

"Only listen to what I can give you in exchange for my life," said the eel man. "I am a powerful spirit. I can be your god of war; I could make you into a mighty warrior."

"I am a man of peace," Tui Qalita replied. "But when I must fight, I need no one to protect me."

"Then let me be your god of love. I can bring you many fine wives."

"I need no one to woo my women for me. I already have the most desirable women in all the islands for my wives," replied Tui Qalita.

"Then let me be your god of sailing," pleaded the eel man. "I will keep you safe from wind and storm when you go out in your canoe."

"I do not fear wind or storm."

"I can give you wealth and riches."

"I am already rich," said Tui Qalita. "No, I want for nothing but the eel I promised the storyteller, and you will do quite nicely."

"Wait!" cried the desperate eel man. "Spare my life and I will give you the most marvelous power that any human could ever possess."

Tui Qalita's grip on the eel tightened, but his interest was caught. "What power?" he asked.

"The power to resist fire," said the eel man gravely. "I can give you the power to walk on hot glowing embers and not be burned."

Tui Qalita was pleased with this thought. "I accept your gift and give you back your life," he told the eel man.

For four days the chief and the eel man gathered firewood. Then they dug a large pit. "We must light a fire in the pit," explained the eel man, "and after that, we must bury ourselves in the embers and bake for four days and four nights. Then my promise will have been fulfilled."

When Tui Qalita returned to his people, they rejoiced. "Where have you been, my chief?" they all asked.

In answer to their questions, Tui Qalita said only, "Make a bed of stones." Servants scrambled to obey his order.

"Build a fire," commanded the chief. This too was done. Darkness was upon them by the time the stones were hot enough to glow red with the heat. "Now summon Dredre the storyteller," commanded the chief, "and gather my people." His order was swiftly carried out, and the visiting storyteller Dredre was given a place of honor among the people. Everyone wondered what had happened to their chief during his mysterious absence and why was he acting so strangely now.

Then before all eyes, Tui Qalita solemnly stepped barefooted across the hot bed of stones. Everyone gasped as back and forth across the red-hot stones he walked, without so much as a burn or a blister to his feet. His people shook their heads in wonder, for never before had a human possessed such power to resist fire. And when he was through, from across the glowing bed of hot coals, the chief met the eye of the storyteller and smiled, as if to say, "A fair price for a story!"

And the astonished storyteller, for once at a loss for words, nodded his head in whole-hearted agreement.

Ever since that time, all Tui Qalita's descendants have been known as the Firewalkers. The story does not tell us whether Dredre ever received his gift of an eel from Tui Qalita, but as long as the Firewalkers possess their power, the storyteller's name shall be remembered. That will be a long, long time, for even today, the Firewalkers of Beqa cross beds of hot glowing stones and suffer no burns and feel no pain.

"If poor people have nothing else, at least they have a tongue with which to defer their debts."
—African folk saying

A Sackful of Stories

[NORWAY]

THERE WAS ONCE A WIDOWER who had an only son. His son's name was Johann, but everyone just called the lad Hans. Father and son were poor shepherds, and spent their days herding a few scrawny sheep. But if the two of them had only rags to wear, more often than not they wore a smile as well.

One day Hans said to his father, "I've decided to get myself a proper job."

"What are you fit to do, Hans?" asked his father. "Herding sheep is all you know."

"It is said that the king is looking for someone to keep his rabbits," replied Hans. "It can't be much harder than keeping sheep, can it?"

"Whoever herds rabbits must be quick and spry, when they take to their heels and run for the woods," warned his father.

"That may be so," agreed Hans, "but it is also said that whoever gets the job shall have the hand of the princess as well."

"Don't go, Hans," begged his father. "Whenever the king needs soldiers for his army, he sets an impossible task and offers up the hand of the princess as a reward. No one succeeds and those who try and fail are sent off to war and never heard from again."

But Hans would not be swayed. "You shall hear from me soon enough, Father, when I send for you from the king's castle." He shook his father's hand, threw his knapsack over his back, and set off at once to try his luck.

Hans was walking through a deep forest, when he came upon a bent old woman who had got her nose caught in a tree stump. However she twisted and turned and tried to pull away, the old woman was still stuck fast.

"Good day to you, mother," said Hans. "I don't know how you got into such a fix, but you look as though you could use some help getting out of it."

"No one has called me 'mother' for a hundred years!" she cried. "Come and help a feeble old woman, for I have been standing here all that time with neither a friend to call on nor a morsel of bread to chew on."

"A hundred years!" exclaimed Hans. "Then it is high time you were set free, poor dear."

"I was chopping firewood when my nose was caught," explained the old woman. "My axe is rusty, but it should serve."

Hans was a strapping big lad and it was quick work for him to take up the axe and free her. "You'll be wanting a bite to eat," he said. "I've only a bit of stale bread, but you are welcome to it."

"After a hundred years," laughed the woman, "an old shoe would taste good!" So the two of them sat down on the stump, and Hans gave her half the bread he had brought with him in his knapsack. When they had eaten the last crumb, the old woman asked, "Now where are you off to, Hans?"

"I'm off to keep the king's rabbits and win the hand of the princess."

"You're a good lad, Hans. I'll send you on your way with a gift that will surely prove useful to you." The old woman reached deep into her pocket and pulled out a little wooden whistle. " 'Tis no ordinary whistle, lad, though it looks common enough. Blow into this whistle and whatever it is you have lost shall come back to you."

" 'Tis a wonderful whistle indeed, mother!" marveled Hans. He thanked her and continued along his way.

When Hans arrived at the castle, the king himself took the shepherd lad out to the courtyard and showed him rabbit hutches made of silver and gold. "Inside these hutches are my rabbits," explained the king. "There are forty of them. Your job is to drive them out to the woods each morning and to bring them home each night. Let me see you do this tomorrow and the job is yours, along with the hand of the princess. But be warned," said the king. "If even one rabbit is missing upon your return, you will be given a different job—that of a soldier in my army for the rest of your life."

The next morning, the king went to see Hans off. When Hans opened the door to the golden hutches, with a whisk of their short tails and a flap of their long ears, all forty rabbits dashed out of the courtyard. They were into the woods before Hans had even reached the castle gates. The king smiled slyly, for he was sure that he had just gotten himself one more soldier for his army.

But Hans smiled too. "Have a good hop about, lads," he called after the rabbits, and then he sauntered happily out the castle gates after them. Hans walked through the forest until he came to a bright clearing, took out his little whistle and blew it. Before he could turn around, rabbits came bounding out of the bushes from all sides.

Hans laughed aloud to see them crowding and milling about his feet. He counted them. There were forty rabbits, not one more or one less.

"Well, then, lads," said Hans to the rabbits, "let's see if I can't turn you into soldiers or the king shall surely make one of me."

That evening, the king and the queen and the princess watched from their balcony for Hans to return, while a large crowd gathered in the courtyard to see the poor shepherd boy dragged off to war. The sun had nearly set when, in the distance, they heard the shrill notes of a whistle.

"Here he comes, poor fellow," came the whispers, for they had seen many a sorry lad taken away to serve in the king's army. In through the gates came the shepherd boy, playing a tune on a little wooden whistle. And then, to the astonishment of the crowd, they saw that he was followed by an army of long-eared soldiers, all marching in formation.

"Fall in!" called Hans. With that, all forty rabbits jumped into their hutches and settled down for the night. Hans looked up to the balcony and saluted the king, bowed to the queen, and winked at the princess. Laughter and applause rose up from the crowd, but in the balcony, the king growled under his breath, "What's this?"

"You must do something," sputtered the queen to the king, "unless you wish to see our daughter wed to the ragged son of a shepherd!"

"Shepherd's son or no," said the princess, "he certainly knows a trick or two."

"Don't worry," the king assured them. "He will not out-fox the fox. I have a plan . . ."

The king hurried down to speak to Hans. "We are quite impressed, my boy," he said.

"Thank you, Your Majesty. Shall we set a date for the wedding?"

"Soon, Hans, soon," said the king, "but before we set a date for the wedding, you must go out three more times. If you can bring back all forty rabbits three days in a row, then and only then may you marry the princess."

"That was not part of the bargain," said Hans, "but if it must be, then it must be."

The next day Hans was busy drilling his rabbits in the forest clearing when he looked up to see the princess. She was dressed as a peasant girl, for the king had sent her in disguise. Though Hans recognized her at once, he didn't let on. "Good day to you, my girl," he called cheerfully.

"And good day to you, my lad," she answered. "I've a favor to ask of you."

"Ask away," he said, "and if I can grant it to such a fair maid, you may be sure that I will."

The princess smiled sweetly. "Then sell me one of your rabbits."

"Ah, that I cannot do," said Hans, "for they are not mine to sell. These rabbits all belong to the king and it will be the worse for me if I lose even one."

"Surely the king won't miss one little rabbit when he has so many others," she replied. "Just one little rabbit . . ." The princess coaxed so prettily that at last Hans said, "I cannot sell you a rabbit, but if you'd care to earn one, that's a different story. Give me a kiss and I shall give you the rabbit of your choice."

"A kiss!" gasped the princess in dismay. But then she thought to herself, "Better to give him one kiss now than to have a ragged shepherd boy for a husband. Besides, what could it hurt? He doesn't know who I really am and by tomorrow he shall be sent to serve as a soldier in a far-off land." So she agreed.

Hans took the princess in his arms and gave her such a sweet kiss that she might even have given him another one, if only he'd asked. But he didn't, so she took her rabbit in her apron and turned homeward. When she approached the edge of the forest, Hans took up his whistle and blew sharply. The rabbit jumped out of her apron and scurried back to its master, leaving the princess to go home empty-handed. When Hans returned to the castle that evening, the king counted up the rabbits, but to no purpose, for every last rabbit was accounted for.

The princess was in tears as she told her mother and father what had happened. "Silly girl," scolded the queen. "Tomorrow I shall go and fetch the rabbit back in a basket."

On the following morning, Hans looked up to see the queen herself, disguised as a farmer's wife, carrying a basket over her arm. Hans knew her at once as the queen, but he didn't let on.

"I am looking to buy a rabbit," she said to Hans. "You must sell me one of yours."

"That I cannot do, mother," he replied.

"I shall pay you well," replied the queen tartly.

"I cannot sell you one at any price, for they belong to the king."

"Believe me," said the queen, "the king would not mind if you gave me just one."

"Even so, it would not be right for me to sell something that does not belong to me. But if you'd care to earn one, I suppose it would do no harm."

"Of course not," said the queen, smiling slyly. "Just tell me what to do."

Now it was Hans's turn to smile as he told her, "All you have to do is get down on all fours and hop like a bunny."

The queen's face turned purple as she said, "I'll do no such thing!"

"If you want a bunny, you will," said Hans. "You might even enjoy it."

The queen fussed and fumed, but then she thought to herself, "There is no one here to see me but this country bumpkin, and he thinks I'm only a farmer's wife. Besides, after tomorrow he shall be serving in the king's army in some far-off land."

"Very well," she frowned. The queen got down on all fours and began hopping about the little clearing until she was red in the face and quite worn out from all that hopping. She looked so silly that Hans almost split his sides laughing.

At last he said, "Oh, good mother, you have earned your rabbit. Only tell me which one you want and I shall fetch it for you." The queen pointed to a fat rabbit and Hans placed it in her basket.

"We shall see who is laughing tomorrow," said the queen as she stomped off toward the castle. But she hadn't gone far when Hans lifted the little wooden whistle to his lips and blew sharply. The rabbit leapt out of her basket. Though the queen stamped her foot and ordered the bunny to return in her most royal voice, the rabbit ran straight back to Hans.

That evening an even bigger crowd gathered in the courtyard to see what kind of a rabbit-keeper Hans was. The king and queen and princess waited and watched from the balcony. Just as the sun was setting, Hans came whistling his way back to the castle, followed by tidy rows of rabbits marching behind. The crowd cheered, the king frowned, the queen scowled, and the princess shook her head in wonder. However many times the king might count them, there were forty rabbits, no more and no less.

"What happened?" growled the king to the queen.

"He . . . he wouldn't sell me a rabbit," admitted the queen rather sheepishly.

"Well, I can see if I want this done right I am going to have to do it myself!" snapped the king.

The very next morning, the king himself, dressed as a peasant and riding a donkey, went to call upon Hans. The shepherd lad recognized him at once, but he didn't let on. Instead he called out, "Good morning, father. What can I do for you?"

"You must sell me a rabbit," said the king gruffly.

"That I cannot do," said Hans, "for they belong to the king. If I sell even one, I shall surely be shipped off into the army."

"I must have one and that is all there is to it," said the king, who was not used to being disobeyed.

"Well, I'm sure you will agree with me that it would be dishonest to sell something that doesn't belong to me. But if you were willing to earn one . . ."

"Yes, yes," said the king. "Just tell me what I must do."

"Do you see that rabbit?" said Hans, pointing to a big brown one. "That is my captain. All you have to do is . . . kiss him once on the place beneath his tail and then I am sure he will agree to go with you."

"That is outrageous!" roared the king.

Hans shrugged and said, "I suppose you can always buy another rabbit at the market."

The king fussed and fumed, but at last he said to himself, "Unless I want this fool for a son-in-law, I shall have to do as he asks. At least he does not know who I am. Besides, by this time tomorrow he shall be serving me as a soldier in a land as far-off as possible!"

"Oh, very well," grumbled the king, and he knelt down and kissed the place beneath the captain's tail. Then the king scooped up the rabbit, tucked him into his coat, and buttoned it up tight. Grumbling and complaining, the king mounted the little donkey and rode off. But as the king approached the castle, Hans lifted the little wooden whistle to his lips and blew sharply. Inside the king's coat the rabbit began to struggle. The king tried to hold onto the wriggling rabbit, but it popped the buttons right off his coat and went scrambling off into the woods.

When Hans returned that evening with all forty rabbits, he smiled and waved to the people gathered in the courtyard. From up in the balcony, the king frowned to see his subjects cheering for the shepherd lad. "How dare they applaud that saucy rogue!" he exclaimed to the queen and the princess. "They shall soon discover that their king is not so easily made a fool of!"

"What do you plan to do?" asked the queen.

"You shall see," said the king.

This time the king had the whole royal family go out to meet Hans. Hans bowed and said, "Your Majesties, I have done as you have commanded. Here are your rabbits. Now may I marry the princess?"

"Soon, Hans, soon," said the king. "There is yet one more task for you to complete."

"That was not part of the bargain," said Hans, "but if it must be, then it must be."

The king clapped his hands once and servants brought out three fine chairs for the royal family to sit upon. The king clapped his hands twice and servants brought out a great block of wood for Hans to stand on, so that everyone in the public square might see and hear him. The king clapped his hands three times and servants brought out a great cloth sack.

"Do you see this sack, Hans?" said the king.

"Yes, Your Majesty," answered Hans.

"For your last task, all you have to do is fill this sack to bursting with stories. Do that and the princess is yours. If you can't, you are mine to do with as I will."

Though everyone present wished Hans good luck, not a one of them dared point out to the king that he had given the lad an impossible task, for how could a cloth sack be filled with stories?

"You may begin," smiled the king.

But if the king was smiling, so was Hans. "Gladly, Your Majesty," he said with a bow. Hans then greeted his audience, cleared his throat, and began, "Listen carefully, good people, for I have many and many a story to put into that sack." Hans told them all about meeting the old woman in the forest and how she had given him the wonderful whistle. He told of coming to the castle to seek work as keeper of the king's rabbits. He told how he had fulfilled the king's terms by bringing home each and every rabbit on the very first day. He even told how the king had broken his promise by demanding that Hans take the rabbits out three more times.

"Is the sack full yet, Your Majesty?" asked Hans.

"Oh, no," replied the king. "Not nearly full."

"Well, then," said Hans, "I shall tell you all about my second day as rabbit-keeper to the king. That morning a pretty peasant girl came to see me, only it wasn't really a peasant girl, but the princess dressed up as a peasant. She begged me to give her a rabbit and when I told her she couldn't have one, she grew so sad that I suggested she might earn one by giving me a kiss. And what do you think she did?"

The princess blushed and said to the king, "Father, surely the sack is full now!"

"Oh, no," said the king jovially, "not a sign of it."

"As I was saying," continued Hans, "the princess puckered up her pretty red lips and gave me a kiss!"

The crowd roared with laughter and even the king joined in.

"Is the sack full yet, Your Majesty?" asked Hans.

"Not even close," the king replied with a chuckle.

"On my third day of keeping rabbits," continued Hans, "who do you think came to see me, but a farmer's wife? Only she wasn't really a farmer's wife, but the queen dressed up as a farmer's wife. She too wanted a rabbit and when I told her she couldn't have one, she became so cross that I suggested she might earn one by hopping about on all fours like a bunny. And what do you think she did?"

The queen blushed and said, "Surely the sack is quite full now, husband!"

"Oh, no," replied the king cheerfully, "not even by half!"

"Well, then," said Hans, "bless me if the queen didn't get down on all fours and hop about like a bunny until she was red in the face!"

Loud guffaws echoed throughout the courtyard. The king slapped his wife on the back and laughed until the tears ran down his cheeks. Hans said to the king, "Is the sack full yet, Your Majesty?"

"No," laughed the king, "it is not!"

"Then I will do my best to fill it," said Hans. "The next day was the very best of all, for who should come to see me but a peasant, only it wasn't a peasant, but the king dressed up as a peasant and riding on a donkey. He too was most anxious to buy a rabbit and when I told him he couldn't have one, he got so very angry that I suggested he might earn one." The smile disappeared from the king's face. Hans paused for a moment, then asked, "Will Your Royal Highness kindly look into the sack and tell me if it is full yet?"

The king blushed and squirmed, but said nothing, so Hans began again, "I told His Majesty that he might earn a rabbit if only he would . . ."

"Enough!" cried the king, leaping to his feet. "Enough! The sack is full! It's full to bursting!"

So Hans stepped down from the great block of wood and the king took his daughter's hand and placed it in that of Hans. Once Hans exchanged the rough clothes of a shepherd for those of a prince, the princess saw that he was as handsome as he was clever and kind. They were married and happily so, for the princess later confessed to Hans that, after that first kiss in the forest, she would have been very sorry to see him sent away. Hans then sent for his father to come and stay with them in the castle. The old man lived to see his son crowned king. King Hans and his wife ruled wisely and well. And it is said that once every year, the great block of wood and the great cloth sack were carried out to the castle courtyard. There King Hans would tell stories to his subjects and, year after year, they never tired of hearing King Hans fill that sack full to bursting.

"Nothing can come out of a sack but what is in it."
—American folk saying

"Truth came to the market and could not be sold:
we buy lies with ready cash."
—African folk saying

Truth and Parable

[YIDDISH]

THE PREACHER OF DUBNO WAS A RENOWNED STORYTELLER. He used this skill to great advantage when he told parables to his congregation. Once he was approached by a learned scholar. "Simple basic truths form the foundation of Judaism," said the scholar to the preacher. "I try to set forth these truths, yet the very same people who are too busy to come hear me recite the Torah flock to the synagogue to hear your stories. Can you explain to me, Rabbi, why this should be? Isn't it better to tell them the truth than to fill their heads with stories?"

"That brings to mind a story," replied the Preacher of Dubno with a smile. "There was once a time when Truth walked about the streets naked. Whenever the people saw him coming, they would cross over to the other side of the street or turn their backs to him. So Truth wandered about sad and alone until one day, when he came upon a great gathering. At the center of the crowd was Parable, dressed in an elegant robe of bright colors. Bitter Truth watched the people push forward to admire Parable and to hear him speak. But when Truth approached, immediately the people frowned and dispersed with a great deal of grumbling.

"As the dejected Truth watched them leave, he said to Parable, 'Why do the people reject me and yet embrace you so warmly? Is it because I am old?'

"Parable smiled and shook his head in reply. 'No, Brother. It is true that you are old, but so am I. In fact, the older I get the better they like me.'

" 'Then why won't they listen to me?' asked Truth mournfully.

" 'I will share my secret with you,' said Parable. 'People simply do not like to meet you naked, face-to-face. If you want people to embrace you as they do me, you must make yourself more attractive to them. Let me help you.'

"Parable lent Truth some of his splendid clothing and soon Truth was dressed as elegantly as his friend. Arm in arm, they strolled down the street. To his surprise and delight, Truth was invited into the homes of the very people who had pushed him aside.

"Ever since that time, Truth and Parable have gone hand in hand and they are made welcome wherever they go.

"And so you see," concluded the Preacher of Dubno, "I do not change the truth, nor try to hide it within my stories. I merely dress it up in beautiful clothing so that people will welcome it into their hearts."

"It all happened long ago, and believe it or not,
it is all absolutely true."
—Traditional Irish opening

Conal Crovi

[SCOTLAND]

IT IS TOLD THAT LONG AGO THERE WAS A KING OF ENGLAND who had three sons. His sons had gone to France to get learning and were on their way home to show their father what they had learned. Along the way, they stopped for food and shelter at the home of Conal Crovi, one of their father's faithful knights.

Conal Crovi welcomed them and gave them the very best of meat and drink. But when the time came for them to lie down, the king's oldest son said haughtily, "Your wife must wait on me, your maid servant must wait on my middle brother, and your daughter must wait on my youngest brother."

"Is this how you repay my hospitality?" said Conal Crovi angrily. He stormed out of the room and called for his three best horses to be saddled. Then he and his wife went on one, his daughter and servant on another, and his son and the maid servant on the third. They rode straightaway to the castle of the King of England. Conal Crovi demanded an audience with the king to tell him of the insulting behavior of his sons, but the king refused to see him.

"The king shall regret having treated Conal Crovi so poorly," came Conal Crovi's hot reply.

For a year and a day, Conal Crovi and his followers lived as outlaws, robbing and harrying the king's men wherever they could. Then one day, a great company of the king's soldiers fell upon Conal Crovi's camp. There was a battle fought and at the end of it, not a king's man was left alive, save for the king's three sons.

"I shall do a work tonight!" said Conal Crovi.

"What is that, my husband?" asked his wife.

"The lifting of the heads from the shoulders of the king's three sons."

With that, Conal Crovi sent for the eldest son and placed his head upon the chopping block. He took an axe in his hands and lifted it to strike.

"Don't, don't," begged the king's eldest son, "and I shall take your part in right and unright forever."

"Very well," said Conal Crovi, "I shall spare you."

Conal Crovi raised up the lad and sent for the middle son. He placed the middle son's head upon the chopping block and lifted his axe to strike.

"Don't, don't," cried the king's middle son, "and I shall take your part in right and unright forever." Conal Crovi spared his life as well.

He then sent for the youngest son and placed his head upon the chopping block. "Don't, don't," pleaded the king's youngest son, "and I shall take your part in right and unright forever."

"Very well, lads," said Conal Crovi. "Tomorrow I shall return you to your father."

But when Conal Crovi arrived at the castle of the King of England, the king said, "Conal Crovi may have my sons in his power, but it shall not be so with me." He had his soldiers seize Conal Crovi and build a gallows in the castle courtyard to hang him. A crowd gathered to watch Conal Crovi die. But when the noose was placed around the poor man's neck, the king's eldest son cried, "I will go in his place!" and the king's middle son cried, "I will go in his place!" and the king's youngest son said, "I will go in his place!"

The King of England frowned and said to his sons, "I have only contempt for the lot of you. Take Conal Crovi then, and never return until you can lift the shame you have brought upon yourselves."

The king's sons left the castle in the company of Conal Crovi. "Do not lose heart, lads," said Conal Crovi. "We shall make a big ship and sail over to Erin. If we bring back the three black whitefaced stallions from the King of Erin, then we will make England as rich as it ever was and you shall win back your father's love."

"But I have heard that the king will not part with those horses, not for pity nor for gold," said the eldest of the sons.

"Then we shall steal them," said Conal Crovi.

He kissed his wife and daughter goodbye and then boarded the ship to cross over to Erin. Upon arriving, they stole into the stable of the King of Erin. There were the magnificent stallions, the king's pride and joy. But when Conal Crovi went to lay a hand upon the stallions, they let out a terrible screech. Three times he tried to capture the horses before they were discovered by the king's guards. Conal Crovi and the King of England's sons were bound and brought before the King of Erin and all his court. The King of Erin laughed and said, "So it is you, Conal Crovi. I do not doubt that you did many a mischief before you thought to steal the black whitefaced stallions of the King of Erin. But you shall not come out of this alive."

"I have been closer to death than I am this night, with a hope yet to live," replied Conal Crovi.

"Now that I doubt!" replied the king. "No man touches the black whitefaced stallions of the King of Erin and lives to tell that tale."

"Then I will tell the tale of how I lived through a harder case than this," said Conal Crovi, "if I get the worth of the telling."

"Tell me the story," said the King of Erin, "and you shall have anything you ask of me, except your life alone."

"That I shall," promised Conal Crovi.

"Hush, then," said the king to his followers. The king's mother was in the hall, tending the fire. "Mother," said the king fondly to the old woman, "let you stir the fire and then we shall hear the tale of Conal Crovi."

Conal Crovi began, "When I was but a young lad, I made a long sea journey. We came to an island and stopped to take in stores. I went ashore to stretch my legs. But when I returned, the ship was gone and I was alone. I found a house and it was there that I saw a woman torn apart with sorrow.

" 'What grieves you so?' I asked her.

"The woman told me, 'The lady of this island is already six weeks dead and must be buried. I am now grieving not only for my lady, but for her brother. He is away and we cannot wait longer for him to bid his sister a final farewell. The burying is to take place today with or without him.'

"The people all gathered at the burying and I was among them," said Conal Crovi. "As I watched them lay a bag of gold beneath the dead lady's head and a bag of silver beneath her feet, I thought to myself that the gold and silver would be of little use to the lady. When I returned to the grave that night, it had not yet been filled in. Down into the grave I went and back up I climbed, with the gold in one hand and the silver in the other. To pull myself out of the grave, I caught hold of a stone, but it came loose and came crashing down upon me. There I was, trapped beneath a great stone, and left to die with only a corpse for company. I ask you, King of Erin, was I not then in a harder case than I am now?"

"That you were," replied the king. "But though you came out of that, you will not come out of this."

"Well, at least then, you must give me the worth of my story."

"What is the worth of it to you, Conal Crovi?" asked the king.

"The eldest son of the King of England married to your oldest daughter and one of the black whitefaced stallions for a dowry."

"That you shall have," agreed the king, "but first tell us how you got out of that grave."

"I will tell the tale," said Conal Crovi, "if I get the worth of the telling."

"You shall have anything you ask of me," promised the king, "except your life alone."

"Well then," continued Conal Crovi, with a nod, "I remained in the grave until the brother of the lady returned from his journey several days later. He insisted upon a final viewing of his sister, even if they must open the grave for him. When I heard the workers digging, I came to my senses and called out to them, 'Take me by the hand!'

" 'Conal Crovi!' cried the brother. 'You did many a mischief before you thought to come and rob the grave of my sister!'

"They were swift in reaching for their swords, but I was swifter still as I fled from the grave. I ran to and fro about the island, not knowing where I should go nor what I should do, when I came upon three lads, all casting lots at the side of a deep hole in the ground. 'What are you doing?' I asked.

" 'A giant has taken our sister,' they told me, 'and we are casting lots to see which one of us shall go down this hole to look for her.'

" 'I have nothing to lose,' said I, 'so I'll cast lots with you.' I did, and it fell upon me to go down and seek her out. They lowered me into that hole in a basket and I found myself in a great dark cave. There I saw the prettiest woman I ever did see and she was winding golden thread off a silver spindle.

"Before I could even speak, there came the thundering footsteps of the giant approaching. Quickly I told her, 'Your brothers are waiting for you at the mouth of the hole. Tomorrow send the basket down to fetch me back. If I am living, 'tis well and good, and if I be not living, then there is no help for it.' I swiftly sent the maiden upon her way and went to hide myself. There was a heap of gold and silver on the other side of the giant's cave, so I hid amidst his treasure. In came the giant with a corpse tied to each of his shoe strings. When he saw the woman was gone, he let out a terrible roar. He howled and cried, but at last he settled down to his dinner. First the giant singed the corpses in the fire and then he ate them.

" 'I shall count my treasure to console myself,' grumbled the giant to himself. But when he reached for his treasure, he set his hand upon my own head.

" 'Conal Crovi!' shouted the giant. 'You did many a mischief before you thought to come and steal my woman. My belly is full tonight, but tomorrow I shall polish my teeth on your bones, you wretch!'

"The big brute was soon fast asleep and snoring. It was then I noticed a great iron meat spit beside the fire. I heated the spit in the fire until it glowed red-hot. The giant's mouth was wide open as he slumbered away; I pushed the hot spit down his throat and leapt aside as he jumped to his feet. As the giant sprang to the far side of the cave, he hit the spit against the wall and it went right through him. I caught up the giant's sword and struck off his head with it. On the morrow, the woman and her brothers came back to fetch me. As they were lowering the basket down the hole, I decided to fill it first with gold and silver from the giant's hoard before getting in myself. But the rope broke beneath the weight of the treasure and down I fell. Taking me for dead, the woman and her brothers left me there amidst the stones and bones, a prisoner in the cave of the giant. Now," said Conal Crovi to the King of Erin, "wasn't I then in a worse case than I am tonight?

"You were indeed," agreed the king. "But though you came out of that, Conal Crovi, you shall not come out of this alive."

"At least you must give me the worth of the story," said Conal Crovi.

"What is the worth of it to you?"

"The middle son of the King of England married to your middle daughter and a black whitefaced stallion for a dowry."

"That you shall have, for I'll not break my word," said the King of Erin. "But first tell us how you escaped from the giant's cave."

"Am I to get the worth of my story?"

"You shall have anything you ask, except your own life," promised the king.

"Well then," continued Conal Crovi, with a nod, "there I was in the cave of the giant, wandering this way and that. I followed a long, dark passage that opened up onto another cave. What did I find there but a woman and she with a naked child on her knee! Though the child cooed and smiled up at her, she was lamenting and crying as though her heart would break. I then saw that she was holding a knife. 'Stay your hand, woman!' I called. 'What are you going to do and why do you weep so sorrowfully?'

'Woe is me,' she cried, 'for I am held prisoner in this cave by three ugly giants. This morning they ordered me to have my own pretty babe dead and cooked for them by the time they come home for dinner. I can't do it and I won't ever do it and surely the giants will kill us both when they return. Oh, what shall I do?'

" 'Hide the child,' I said. 'I see three dead men hanging from ropes over yonder. I will cut down one of them and take his place. You cook up the corpse instead of the babe.'

"She did as I told her and when the giants came home calling for their supper, she served them up a stew made from the corpse. But one of the giants said, 'This is not the tender flesh of a babe.'

" 'No, it is not,' agreed the second giant.

" 'It is,' said the woman. 'Tis the flesh of the babe.'

" 'I will go and cut a steak from one of those three dead men and we will compare,' said the third giant.

"With a great carving knife, he came over to where I hung with the two corpses and he began feeling the bodies. 'This one is too tough,' said the giant, 'and this one is too lean.' He then took a firm hold of me and said, 'Ah, now this one is just right!' "

Conal Crovi turned to face the King of Erin and said, "Now I ask you, king of Erin, was I not in a harder case than I am here tonight?"

"Upon my honor, you were," exclaimed the King of Erin. "Though you came out of that, Conal Crovi, you shall not come out of this alive."

"At least give me the worth of the story."

"What is the worth of it to you?" asked the king.

"The youngest son of the King of England married to your youngest daughter and a black whitefaced stallion as a dowry."

"That you shall have," promised the King of Erin. "Now, Conal Crovi, I would hear the end of your story. Tell us how you freed yourself from the clutches of the giant and I will grant you anything but your life, and had I not sworn years ago to take the life of any who so much as touched my black whitefaced stallions without my leave, I would have granted you even that."

"If you will not give me my life, then I will ask for nothing else; I have what I came for. But . . . for the sake of the story," said Conal Crovi, with a shrug, "I shall finish."

The storyteller was applauded by the courtiers of the king, who were anxious to hear the end of his story. The king raised his hands for silence, and Conal Crovi continued, "Well then, it was all I could do to stay silent as the giant cut a large slice of flesh from my flank, but I held in the screeches that were bursting to get out while the giants cooked up the meat, ate their dinner, and went to bed. Soon they were fast asleep and snoring, but I was too weak to come down, for my life's blood was flowing from my wounds. Just as I was thinking of closing my eyes forever, the woman came and cut me down.

"I said to her, 'Run as quickly as you can and get the flaming sword of light I see hanging on the wall. Take it and cut off the head of the giants as they sleep.'

"She ran off and came quickly back with the sword. Then, as brave and strong as any man, she raised it over her head with her two hands and cut off the heads of the sleeping giants.

" 'Now I'll die easy,' I said to her.

" 'You'll not die at all,' she told me, 'for I'll carry you to the giant's cauldron of cure, and it will heal your wounds.' "

"The dear woman lifted me up onto her back and carried me off to where the giants kept their cauldron of cure. As she raised me up to the edge of the cauldron, the sight was leaving my eyes and the death-faint was spreading over my brain. But she lowered me into the healing water, and no sooner did it touch my skin, than I felt my strength coming back into me.

"The woman and I still knew not how to get out of the cave. We searched the innermost end of the cave until we found a pathway leading to a tunnel. We followed that narrow path until we saw a ray of light. The light came from a small opening that led through the rock to a harbor, where the giants kept a ship. We loaded the ship with the dead giants' treasure and we sailed, the woman, the babe, and I, until we came to an island. There the woman and the babe were taken from me and I was left to find my way home as best I could. Many a mile I have traveled and many a mischief I have done since that time, but for all that I have no regrets," said Conal Crovi with a shrug. "When it comes to ways of dying, I think that being eaten alive is a far worse death than death by hanging. And though you mean to hang me tonight, King of Erin, there is as yet no rope about my neck."

"There shall be before I am finished with you, Conal Crovi, but 'tis a pity indeed that such a fine storyteller must die."

Just then the mother of the king sprang to her feet and cried out, "This brave man shall not die—not by order of the King of Erin!"

"What do you mean by this, Mother?" frowned the king.

The old woman turned to Conal Crovi and asked, "Was it really you then in the cave of the giant?"

"I could show you the scars to prove it," said Conal Crovi.

"Well, I was there too, for I am the woman you saved," she exclaimed, "and my son the King of Erin was that babe."

All of the company was thunderstruck. The King of Erin gasped, and when he came back to his senses, he rushed over to Conal Crovi and with his own hands cut loose the bonds that held him. The king said, "I'll not insult you by saying your life is yours, Conal Crovi. Instead I'll say that my life, my castle and all that's in it are yours!"

Conal Crovi and the sons of the King of England were feasted for twenty nights and twenty days. Then Conal Crovi returned to England with the three young princes. They traveled fast and they traveled far until at last they came within sight of their father's castle. With them they brought fine and worthy wives and the priceless black whitefaced stallions as dowries.

So pleased was the King of England that he lifted the scorn from his sons and from that day onward, Conal Crovi was held in the highest esteem by both the King of England and the King of Erin. In the years that followed, more than once Conal Crovi was called to the kings' courts to entertain them with the tales of his many mischiefs—from the days both before and after he thought to steal the black whitefaced stallions of the King of Erin.

"Good words cost no more than bad."
—American folk saying

The Gossiping Clams

[SUQUAMISH (NATIVE AMERICAN)]

LONG, LONG AGO, WHEN THE WORLD WAS NEW and the animals could talk, clams were the most talkative of all. And no wonder, for their mouths stretched the full length of their bodies. The clams not only loved to talk, they told stories as well. Some of the stories were true and some were not.

"Did you know," said one clam to Eagle, who was eating a fish on the beach, "that Raven says he is a much better hunter than you?"

Eagle's feathers ruffled in annoyance. "Perhaps that is true," scoffed Eagle, "if picking at carrion can be called 'hunting'."

Once when Otter came down to the beach to splash in the water, another clam said to him, "I don't think you make yourself foolish when you come down to play in the waves."

"Who said I look foolish?" demanded Otter.

"I really shouldn't say," said the clam, "but you might go and ask Beaver. Beaver thinks that everyone should work as hard as she does."

It wasn't long before all the animals were quarreling with each other, and all because of the stories that the clams were spreading. Raven finally got so tired of all that gossiping that he called a council meeting and invited all the animals. Bear, Eagle, Mink, Otter, Wolf, and many others came. It was decided at that meeting that, in order to preserve the peace, a way must be found to put a stop to these unkind stories.

"Beaver," said Raven, "we cannot decide how to punish the clams. You are a good worker. We know that you will keep working until you discover a solution, so we have chosen you to rid us of this problem."

Beaver thought and thought, and at last she thought of a plan. She gathered up armloads of the clams—every last one of them—and carried them to the edge of the water.

"What are you doing?" they asked in alarm.

"You shall see soon enough," replied Beaver. "Never again will you spread your mean-spirited tales."

Beaver waited there until the tide went out and then, quickly, she buried each and every one of those clams in the sand. The clams were outraged! When Bear came down to walk along the beach, one of the clams opened its mouth to tattle on Beaver. But as soon as it did, sand and water ran in. The clam sputtered and spit out the water. Again it opened its mouth, but as soon as it did, the sand and water ran into it, and all the poor clam could do was spit out the water and close its mouth.

Even today, if you walk along the beach at low tide, you might see a little spurt of water squirting up from beneath the sand here and there. That is just a clam spitting out the water it swallowed when it opened its mouth to gossip!

"Time never ends.
There is no end to any time."
—Yoruba ritual opening

The Endless Story

[SPAIN]

THERE WAS ONCE THE HEADMAN OF A VILLAGE who had a daughter named Rosita. She was lovely to look upon and of extraordinary intelligence. And she had come of an age to marry. Stories of Rosita's charms traveled far, so that suitors came from miles around to see if the tales were true. They were indeed; one and all were smitten. But the headman, too, doted upon the girl and had promised Rosita that he would never force her to marry against her will.

"It would be lovely to have a husband who was young and handsome and rich," Rosita told her father, "but if he were all those things and a fool too I would refuse him. I shall have no fool for a husband."

It was indeed a problem to find a husband whose intelligence was the equal of his daughter's. The headman spent many sleepless nights until at last he thought of a test to determine who would be a suitable suitor for his clever daughter.

"Rosita," he said, "you enjoy a good story, do you not?"

"You know I do, Father."

"Have you ever heard a story without an end?"

"I have heard many and many a story, Father," she replied, "but I have never heard a story without an end."

"Let us have a contest then," suggested her father. "The one who can tell an endless story shall be the one who wins your hand."

"That is a story I would like to hear," said Rosita with a smile.

So the headman announced the contest. It was to be held in the main square of the village. When the day came, the square was crowded with people. Hundreds of suitors, both young and old, rich and poor, had come from near and far to try to win fair Rosita's hand with a story. No time was lost in getting started, for there were many stories to hear.

One after another, the rivals presented themselves to Rosita, thinking to tell a story with no end. Some of their stories lasted for days, others for weeks. But every one of them, despite all claims, told a tale that eventually came to an end. One young man told a story that lasted for three months, but eventually he, too, ran out of ideas. Some got up to tell a story and were stopped short by the taunts and jeers of the crowd. Still others were drowned out by roars of laughter until they, too, stepped down.

Rosita and her father had nearly given up hope of hearing an endless tale when a man, still dusty from the road, stepped forward. "I have a tale for the *señorita,*" he said.

"Who are you," asked Rosita, "to think you can succeed where a hundred have already failed?"

"I am only Miguel, a wandering storyteller, *señorita,* but I have many and many a tale to tell—and perhaps even one without end."

"Tell it then, Miguel," she said, "and I will listen."

The storyteller bowed to the lady and began, "Long, long ago there lived a king called Oba of Idu. He was a cruel tyrant and his subjects had to obey his every whim or be put to death. One day Oba of Idu ordered his subjects to build him a place to store grain. They toiled day and night; laborers died like dogs at the foot of the great mud walls, and still the work went on. At the end of ten years, the high walls of the granary stretched up to the sky and out of sight.

"The cruel king then ordered his soldiers to seize all the grain in the country, leaving his subjects to starve. It took even more time for the king's soldiers to fill the granary than it had taken to build it. From season to season, year to year, the soldiers labored without ceasing.

"Then came a time of terrible drought, when crops withered and cattle died of starvation. The people too were starving, so they went to the king and begged him for a bit of the grain he had stolen and stored away. But Oba of Idu had a heart of stone; he refused to help his people.

"Yet God must have been watching over them. The very next day Oba of Idu's granary was invaded by an army—an army of birds. While it is true that the granary stretched to the sky, there was one tiny hole high up in the wall. That hole was just big enough to let the tiny sparrows in, one at a time. So one at a time that army of birds flew in through the hole and then each bird flew out again with a grain of corn in its beak. The birds delivered the corn to the hungry villagers and there was nothing the greedy king could do to stop them."

The crowd of listeners gave a loud cheer as Miguel went on to dance out the graceful movements of the birds with his arms. He sang,

"Flying up
flying down
it took a grain of corn.
Flying up
flying down
it took a grain of corn."

Now the audience joined in and took up the storyteller's refrain. They all began to chant,

"Flying up
flying down
it took a grain of corn.
Flying up
flying down
it took a grain of corn."

On and on it went, until the headman finally rose and impatiently asked Miguel, "How much longer will the birds be going in and out and carrying away the grain?"

"O *señor*!" smiled Miguel, "the quantity of corn was immeasurable and the number of birds countless and they have as yet cleared only a small portion of the king's granary . . ."

Rosita's father frowned, but Rosita laughed aloud and said, "Father, let us not waste any more time. Clearly Miguel has begun an endless story. We must not let him go on if you would live to see your grandchildren."

A smile spread slowly across her father's face. With a loud guffaw, he said, "Miguel, come and take your wife! You are a man of great intelligence and a fine storyteller indeed. Who would ever have thought that there could be an endless story?"

Miguel took Rosita's hand and smiled into her dark, shining eyes. "I have an even better one . . ." he began.

"We have the rest of our lives for you to tell it to me," said Rosita.

"Better to show you than to tell you," said the storyteller, "for it is the never-ending story of my love for you."

Miguel gave up his wandering and stayed with Rosita. They had many children and grandchildren. Over the years, Miguel told them many and many a story, but none so sweet as the never-ending story of his love for the fair Rosita.

"There is no shame in being silent
if you have nothing to say."
—Russian folk saying

The Silent Princess

[TURKEY]

ONCE UPON A TIME, THERE LIVED A PASHA who had an only son. The young prince's favorite toy was a golden ball. One day, as he was sitting in the garden, he noticed an old woman with an earthen pitcher coming to draw water from the well. Without thinking, the boy caught up his ball and flung it straight at the pitcher, which broke into a hundred pieces. Shaking her fist at the boy, the old woman cried, "May you be punished by falling in love with the silent princess!"

The young prince paid no heed to her words—indeed he forgot them altogether. But as time passed and he grew to be a young man, the memory of the old woman's curse came back to mind. "Who is the silent princess," he wondered, "and why should it be a punishment to fall in love with her?" He asked himself over and over again until he could think of nothing else. He could not sleep, he could not eat, and finally he grew ill.

When questioned by his father, the prince confessed the cause of his illness. The pasha, who was a wise man, told him, "Go, my son. Go into the world in search of this silent princess and perhaps you will find your peace."

So the young prince rose from his bed and set out upon the dusty road. He traveled through dense forests and across sandy deserts. He traversed raging rivers and salty seas. He wandered until he was no more than skin and bones and his princely garments hung in tatters. He wandered until he was so weak that he almost forgot the object of his quest. Until one fateful day.

It was at the foot of a shining mountain that the prince felt his heart begin to beat with joy. The numbness brought on by the hardships of his journey fell away. The prince knew in his heart that he was nearing the end of his quest. He came to a small village and asked an old man, "Have you heard of the silent princess, grandfather?"

"Indeed I have," replied the old man. "She lives with her father, the sultan, in a marble palace at the top of yon mountain."

"Will you kindly tell me the quickest way to get there?"

"Up and up is the quickest and the only way," replied the old man, "but 'tis also the quickest way to lose your head. Many young men before you have come in search of the silent princess, thinking to make her speak and win her hand in the bargain; they have all paid with their lives."

"Why will she not speak?" asked the prince.

"Her father wishes to see his only daughter wed before he dies, but she refuses to marry any man who is not as clever as she. She has proclaimed that any man clever enough to make her speak shall have her as his bride. To discourage her suitors, she requires that they pay for failure with their lives. Still they come, for each believes himself to be the one who will break her silence. But she holds her tongue and they lose their heads. If you are truly clever," warned the old man, "you will turn around and go back to wherever it is you came from."

"Better a quick death," replied the prince, "than to pine away slowly." The young prince thanked the old man and began to climb the steep sides of the mountain. As he neared the top, he paused in horror, for the ground was white with dead mens' skulls. "Ah, well," said the young prince to himself, "a man can die but once."

At last, just as the sun sank down toward the western rim of the world, he came to a magnificent palace at the top of the mountain. "I have come to speak with the princess," said the prince to the sultan.

"You are a handsome young man in spite of your rags," said the sultan, shaking his head in pity. "Did you take note of the sun-bleached bones upon the mountainside, my son? I would not see your bones among them; turn back while you still can."

"Some day a man shall break the silence," said the prince. "Why should I not be the one? Besides, I have already lost my heart to the princess; if I cannot have her hand, she may have my head, for what good is a head without a heart to guide it?"

"So be it," said the sultan. "My servant will take you to the princess and remain to serve as witness."

The prince soon found himself standing before the silent princess, who was seated on a cushion and shrouded in seven veils. He bowed to her, but did not speak. Instead he settled onto another cushion and sat in silence himself. After a time, the prince turned to the witness and said, "Won't you tell me a tale to pass the time?"

"I am not here to speak, but to listen," replied the witness.

"Very well," said the prince, "then I shall tell a tale and you can listen." With that, he launched into his story.

"Three companions each sought the hand of a beautiful princess. She rejected all three, telling them that they must first go out into the world and see what they might learn. She promised to marry the most clever of the three upon their return. They traveled far and wide and they learned many things. One of them learned to see to the ends of the earth. Another learned the secret of flight and had woven a carpet which, in the wink of an eye, could fly to the ends of the earth. The third learned the secret of life and could revive the dead.

"One day, the three sat down to rest. To pass the time, the young man who could see to the ends of the earth looked into the palace of the princess. He went pale. 'The princess is dead!' he cried. 'Even now they are carrying her to her grave!'

" 'Hurry!' said the second. 'Get on my carpet and we will go to her.' The three friends sat down on the magic carpet, and in an instant it carried them to her palace. They said to the king, 'Do not bury your daughter, sire. We can revive her.'

"The one who knew the secret of life worked his art and soon the princess began to breathe and the color returned to her cheeks. Amidst the great rejoicing of her family and friends, the three young men began to argue.

"The one who could see to the ends of the earth said, 'If it were not for me, the princess would have been buried by now, and we would still be wandering unaware in a far-off land. She belongs to me.'

"The one who could fly to the ends of the earth said, 'If it had not been for me, the princess would now be in her grave, for we would never have arrived in time to revive her. She belongs to me.'

"Then the one who knew the secret of life said, 'If it were not for me, the princess would be long dead, for it was I who brought her back to the land of the living. I have the greatest right to her.'

At this point in his story, the young prince fell silent. The witness, though he had been forbidden to speak, was so caught up in the tale that he asked, "What happened next? Who married the princess?"

"What would your decision be?" asked the prince of the witness.

The witness shook his head and frowned. "It is a difficult matter to decide. Only men of judgment would know. We must ask them tomorrow morning."

"You forget," the prince reminded him, "that tomorrow morning I will be dead. I do not wish to go to my grave without the answer."

The silent princess was no longer able to contain herself. She sprang to her feet and cried, "Fools! Isn't it obvious? The princess belongs to no one but herself. But of course she would choose to marry the man who had given her life."

"Thank you for your decision, my princess," said the young prince. "I am sure that you have answered correctly."

Beneath her seven veils, the princess stiffened and her cheeks grew hot as she realized that she had just fallen into the prince's cunning trap.

At dawn the king arrived with the royal executioner, who seized the prince's arm to lead him away to the chopping block. But the witness stopped him and said, "Wait. Last night the princess spoke."

"Is this true?" asked the king of his daughter.

But the princess refused to utter another word. All she could be prevailed upon to do was to make signs to her father that the man who would wed her must induce her to speak three times. And she smiled to herself beneath her seven veils as she thought of the impossibility of that! The prince merely bowed low to the princess and smiled, "Until tomorrow night then, princess."

The next evening, towards sunset, the prince presented himself at the palace. A different servant led the prince to the chambers of the princess, then remained to serve as witness. Again the prince sat in silence. At length he turned to the witness and said, "Won't you tell me a tale to pass the time?"

The witness replied, "I am not here to speak, but to listen."

"Very well," said the prince, "then I shall tell a tale and you can listen." With that, the prince began his story.

"A nobleman, his wife, and his coachman were traveling. They found themselves in the middle of nowhere at nightfall. They spent the night at the side of the road. At midnight they were attacked by a band of highwaymen. The brigands robbed them and beheaded both men, but spared the woman. Although she knew that it was hopeless, the poor widow placed the severed heads back upon the bodies of the men. Then she fell to her knees and wept and prayed until dawn. Allah heard her prayers and, when daylight came, the men opened their eyes and sat up. But, to her dismay, the woman discovered that she had placed the servant's head upon her husband's body and her husband's head upon the servant's body. The two men began to argue, each one maintaining his right to the noblewoman as her husband.

" 'She is my wife,' said the one with the nobleman's head and the servant's body.

" 'She is *my* wife,' said the one with the servant's head and the nobleman's body."

At this point in his story, the young prince shrugged and fell silent. But the witness had become so involved that he forgot himself. "You can't stop there. Tell me, to whom did the noblewoman belong?"

"It is a difficult question," said the prince. "What do you think?"

"I do not know," admitted the witness. "That would be for a man of learning to decide. Tomorrow let us go to the sultan's advisor and ask."

"You forget," the prince reminded him, "that there shall be no tomorrow for me, as I am to be beheaded at dawn."

"Fools!" cried the princess, jumping to her feet. "Isn't it obvious? The woman belongs to no one but herself. But she would certainly go with the one who had her husband's head, for therein dwelt the memories of the life they had shared."

"Thank you for your decision, my princess," said the prince. "I am sure you have answered correctly."

Again the princess was furious with herself for becoming so caught up in the tale as to break her silence. "Never again," she promised herself, "though this young man could charm a snake with his stories."

The next evening found the prince and yet a third witness sitting in cold silence in the chamber of the princess. Once again the prince asked the witness for a story and was refused, so he began a story of his own. "There were once three men, a woodcarver, a tailor, and a scholar, who set out together to see the world. They were in a deep, dark forest when night fell. They made their camp, but for safety's sake, they decided to take turns keeping watch for wolves and brigands. The woodcarver took the first watch. To pass the time, he found a piece of wood lying near their camp and carved it into the statue of a woman. He worked feverishly until he finished. The woodcutter then roused the tailor and fell into an exhausted sleep.

"The tailor rubbed the sleep out of his eyes and sat by the fire to take his turn at the watch. He looked up to see a beautiful woman nearby. He stood speechless for an instant before he reached out to touch her hand. To his amazement, he found that she had been fashioned out of wood.

" 'Ah! I can make you more beautiful still,' he said. He fetched scissors, needle, thread, and a bolt of his finest cloth. All throughout his watch, the tailor cut and draped and stitched until the statue was clothed in a lovely gown. The statue was now breathtaking in its beauty. Satisfied with his work, the tailor woke the scholar.

"When the scholar arose and saw the wooden maiden standing there, he fell on his knees and lifted his hands in ecstasy. 'Surely such a one is not meant to live without a soul,' thought the scholar, and he prayed with all his might that life should be breathed into it.

His prayer was heard and the beautiful maiden came to life. For the rest of the night, the scholar taught her to speak. But all three men loved her and each claimed the right to marry her.

The woodcarver said, 'I gave her shape. I have the greatest right to her.'

"The tailor said, 'I dressed her and made her beautiful. My contribution is as great as yours.'

"The scholar said, 'I prayed and asked that life be breathed into her. I taught her to speak. I have the greatest right.' "

At this point, the young prince fell silent. "Finish your story," demanded the witness. "To whom did the maiden belong?"

The young prince turned to the silent princess and said, "What is your opinion, princess?"

There was a long silence and then, beneath her seven veils, the princess sighed, then smiled, then laughed aloud. "She belonged to no one but herself, but if I were her, I would go to the one who had given me life and taught me to speak."

"Thank you, princess," said the young prince, taking her outstretched hand. "I am sure that you have answered correctly," he said with a smile, "and I promise to do my best to prove it to you."

After the wedding feast was over, they sent for the old woman whose pitcher the prince had broken so long ago. The old woman lived in the palace and became nurse to their many children. The prince and the princess lived happily ever after, for he kept his wife entertained with his stories and she, silent no more, never tired of telling her husband of her love for him.

"The sultan's miracles are those of his own telling."
—Turkish folk saying

Backing Up a Story

[CHINA]

THERE WAS ONCE A MAN WHO WAS KNOWN FOR HIS WILD STORIES. He bragged to his friends, he boasted to his relatives, and he lied to his wife. There was nothing mean-spirited about his tales; he simply enjoyed a good story and, if he told that story often enough, he would even come to believe in it himself.

"You had better harness your tongue, old man," warned his wife, "for sooner or later one of your stories will come home to roost."

"Of course, you are right, my dear," he would say good-naturedly. "Why, I once heard of a man who stretched the truth so far that it reached from Canton to Peking!"

One day the old man returned from the next village, where he had been visiting relatives. His wife had never seen him so agitated.

"Whatever is the matter, husband?" she asked.

He held his head in his hands and moaned, "You were right, my dear. I have been caught in my own trap. I told my relatives that even though I was not a rich man, I had three precious treasures worth far more than anything money could buy."

"Yes, go on," urged his wife.

"I told them that I had a bullock which could run 1,000 *li* a day."

"You didn't! No animal can travel that fast," said his wife. "What else did you say?"

"I said that I had a rooster which crowed at the beginning of each watch, day and night . . ."

"No! And the third treasure?"

"That, I fear is the biggest lie of all. I told them that I have a dog who is so clever he can read and write!"

"Well, look at the bright side, old man. They live far enough away so that they will never discover what big lies you told."

"That is the problem!" cried the miserable old man. "My brother and his son have promised to come here tomorrow to see these marvels with their own eyes. What if they journey all this way only to find that I was merely boasting? If only I could find a way out of this embarrassing situation, I would never tell another story again!"

"Never mind," clucked his wife. "Tomorrow you must hide yourself in the shed, old man. Just leave the rest to me."

The next day, the old man's brother and nephew came calling, still covered with dust from the road. But when they asked for the old man, his wife said, "I'm sorry, but you have just missed him; he has gone to Peking."

"When do you expect him back?" they asked in dismay.

"In eight or nine days," she replied.

"Only eight or nine days to make such a long journey!" exclaimed his brother. "How can that be?"

"He is riding our bullock," she shrugged. "He's very fast, you know."

"We understand that you also have a very special rooster," ventured the old man's brother.

At that very moment, by a stroke of luck, the rooster crowed.

"That's him now," said the wife. Thinking quickly, she added, "Did my husband tell you that he also crows whenever a visitor arrives? He is better than a watchdog."

"If you need a watchdog," said her brother-in-law, "why don't you use that marvelous dog of yours? We understand that he is very learned. In fact, we have come all this way to have him read for us."

"I am sorry," said the old woman, "but we are so poor that we had to let our dog go to the city, where he keeps a school to support us."

Her husband's relatives were so impressed that they were halfway home before it occurred to them to wonder. And so the old man was saved from disgrace by his clever wife.

"That's the end of that," said his wife, "since you did promise never to tell another wild story again."

"Quite right, my dear," said the old man. "Or I might end up like the old man who told such terrible lies that they made him row all the way down the Yang-zte River in a rice bowl."

The moral of this story is quite simple: If you insist on inventing stories, you had better marry an even better storyteller to back you up.

"Cocks crow, but hens deliver the goods."
—Irish folk saying

III

ONE FOR THE ONE WHO TAKES IT TO HEART

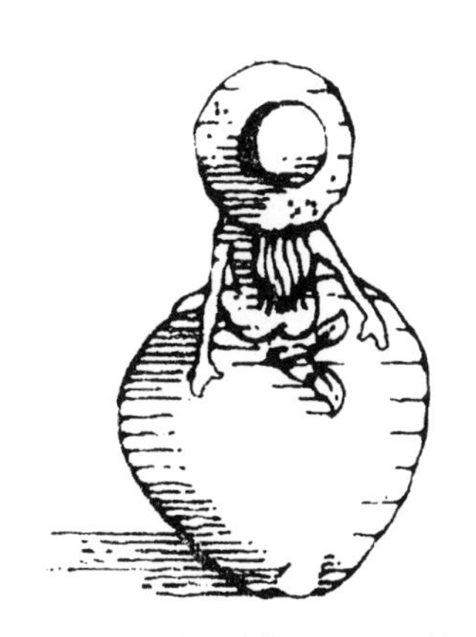

"There are no people a thousand years old,
but there are words a thousand years old."
—Mongolian folk saying

The Storytelling Stone

[SENECA (NATIVE AMERICAN)]

LONG, LONG AGO THERE LIVED IN A SENECA VILLAGE a boy whose parents had died when he was very young. He was taken in by a woman who was herself childless. When he was old enough, the boy's foster mother gave him a bow and arrows and said, "Now you must learn to hunt and earn your keep. Take this bow into the forest and bring back some meat."

The boy set off into the woods and hunted all day long. At first he was clumsy with the bow and arrows, but before the day was through, he had killed a string of birds to take home to his foster mother. "Good," she told him. "Tomorrow you will do even better."

The next day did prove to be an even better day for hunting and the boy brought home many more birds. "Some day," his foster mother told him, "you will be a great hunter and bring home deer and bear."

Each day the boy hunted and at evening he returned with the day's kill, a long string of birds for his foster mother. Each day he ventured farther and farther into the woods in search of game. One day, when it was time to stop for his midday meal, the boy found himself deep in the forest. Up ahead he saw a clearing with a great stone in its center. The boy climbed up on top of the stone, set his string of birds beside him, and began to eat his meal of parched corn and dried berries. It was then that he heard a voice and it asked, "Shall I tell you stories?"

The startled boy looked all around; there was no one to be seen. But as soon as he went back to his meal, again the strange voice asked, "Shall I tell you stories?"

The boy looked about in every direction, but he could see no one. This time, he set his meal to one side and watched and waited for the voice to speak again.

"Shall I tell you stories?" said the voice again.

It was then that the boy realized the voice was coming from the stone on which he sat. Though the boy had never heard a stone speak before, he was not frightened. He asked the stone, "What does this mean—to tell stories?" For at that time, there were no stories in the world.

The stone replied, "It is to tell of the things that happened a long time ago."

"I think I would like that," replied the boy.

"Then give me your birds and I will tell you stories," said the stone.

The boy readily agreed and the stone began. It told stories from the time when the people lived up in the sky. It told stories of the earth's creation. It told stories of long, long ago, when the animals could speak. As soon as one story was finished, the stone began another. The boy sat enthralled, forgetting his hunger, too caught up in the stories to notice that the shadows were growing long in the forest. At last the storytelling stone said, "Now it is time to rest."

"May I come tomorrow?" asked the boy anxiously.

"Yes," replied the stone, "but tell no one of our meeting."

In the fading light, the boy was able to kill a bird or two on his way home. "Is this all you bring me?" asked his foster mother. "Why so little, when you have already shown your skill as a hunter?"

"The birds are now afraid of me," was the boy's excuse. "I must travel farther to find them."

The next morning the boy killed many birds as he made his way back to the storytelling stone, but he could think only about the stories he would hear that day. When he arrived in the clearing, the great stone said, "Give me your birds and I will tell you stories."

Eagerly the boy climbed up, placed the long string of birds upon the stone as his offering, then sat with his head bowed and his eyes closed as the stone told him its stories. It was twilight before the storytelling stone said, "Now it is time to rest."

The boy hurried home, managing to kill a few birds in the last light of day. But again his foster mother frowned at his meager catch. Something was not right. So the next morning she asked an older boy from the village to follow her foster son as he hunted that day. The other boy followed at a distance, watching as the younger boy killed many birds. The older boy stopped now and then to kill a few birds himself, but he never lost track of the boy he had been sent to follow. When the younger boy stepped into a clearing, the other boy hid behind some trees and watched him climb up on a big stone. From his hiding place, the older boy could hear voices, but he could not see who was speaking. Puzzled, he stepped out of the woods and asked, "Who are you speaking to? What are you doing here?"

"I am listening to stories," replied the boy.

"What are stories?"

"They tell about things that happened long ago. Give the stone your birds, then sit down beside me and listen."

The older boy joined the younger and the two of them sat listening until the sun disappeared behind the trees. The stone announced, "Now it is time to rest." On their way home, both boys killed as many birds as they could, but they were only able to bring home a few.

Now each day two boys brought their birds to the clearing and offered them to the stone in exchange for stories. The foster mother told several men in the village, "They kill more birds than they bring home. Will you not follow them into the woods and see what it is that they do each day?"

So the next day two men followed the boys to the storytelling stone and watched them place their long strings of birds upon it. They watched the boys listening with heads bowed. They heard the strange voice speaking. At last the men stepped out of hiding and they said, "What are you doing here? Who are you talking to?"

Soon the two men were seated upon the storytelling stone, as enthralled by the stories as the boys. When the last tale was told, the stone said, "Tomorrow you must bring all your people to hear my stories. Tell them that they must bring a gift in exchange for the stories. Go now and prepare them."

So the four hurried back and delivered the stone's message to the chief. Early the next day, every man, woman, and child in the village bore a gift as they walked to the clearing, made their offerings, and sat at the foot of the great stone. The storytelling stone said, "I will tell you stories of things that happened long ago. You must listen well, for when I am finished, it will be for you to remember and tell each other these stories."

The stone began early in the day and told one story after another. It spoke of the world when it was new. It told them stories of the first people, the sky people. It told stories of the animals who could talk, and how the world came to be. At last, when night had nearly come, the stone fell silent. The people waited. Then it spoke for the last time. "You must keep these stories until the end of time," it told them. "Tell them to your children and your children's children. Whenever a story is told, you will give a gift to the storyteller, for you can no longer look to me for your stories. I am done."

From this stone came all the stories of the world. Since that time, the storyteller has been welcomed wherever he goes. And since that time, the winter nights no longer seem so cold and dark, for the people have their stories to warm their hearts and shorten the night.

"When fire burns in the soul,
the tongue cannot remain silent."
—Old English folk saying

The Head of Donn Bó

[IRELAND]

THEY TELL A TALE IN ERIN of a shining youth named Donn Bó. Young though he was, Donn Bó was renowned throughout Erin as a singer of songs and the best teller of tales in all the land. When he sang, even the nightingale stopped to listen and when he told stories, even the willow would weep. And such tales to tell! Donn Bó could recite stories of love to melt a heart of ice or tales of bogles and banshees to chill the blood. But he was best known for his "king stories." Donn Bó could tell tales of every king who ever reigned in Erin, from the earliest kings to those who were ruling in his own day.

Now it happened one time that Fergal, the King of Erin, was waging a fierce war against the King of North Leinster. When King Fergal went to assemble his army, one by one each fighting man had told him, "If Donn Bó go with thee, I too will go." Now Donn Bó's mother was a widow, and he had never gone for a day or a night out of his mother's house. Though the old woman wept bitter tears, the bard agreed to accompany his king and his countrymen.

But the expedition began badly. Fergal's guides led him astray and when they pitched their tents that night, it was too near to the hut of a leper. In his outrage, the leper cursed them soundly. And on the night before the battle, a storm came upon them like the vengeance of the Lord, dampening their spirits as well as the sky. So the fighting men went to their bard and said, "Tell us a story, Donn Bó, and sing us a song."

But Donn Bó replied, "No, my friends, for on this night you must make merry; go laugh at the jests of the king's buffoon. You have my word that tomorrow at this hour, wherever you and I shall be, I will tell my finest stories to you."

At dawn the Leinstermen came to meet Fergal and the battle they fought was the fiercest that ever was fought in Erin. Many heroes fell that day. That evening, with the battle behind them, the weary warriors returned to their camp heartbroken, for their king was nowhere to be found and they feared he had been taken by their foes or had fallen in the fray. The soldiers ate their meat, then lifted their cups and dropped a tear for the King of Erin.

"Where is Donn Bó," called the champion of Munster, "that he may lift our spirits and weave for us the word-spell he promised us yesternight?"

But if their king was missing, so was their minstrel. They searched among the living for their warrior bard, but could not find him. So they determined to search for his body among the dead. With torches to light their way in the dark, the soldiers returned to the bloody battlefield. It was there that they found him, and their missing king as well. The shining youth lay dead, his fair young body stretched across the body of the King of Erin, for he had died defending his fallen chief. But the young minstrel's head was nowhere to be found; it had been struck from his shoulders by a single cruel blow and had rolled away among the rushes.

As the soldiers of Erin stood with their heads bowed in grief, there rose up in the air all about them a sad sweet sound. Amidst the eerie stillness of the battlefield, like the rustling of the rushes, came the faint whispers of the dead. Then came the wild, clear note of the battle-march, played by the long-cold hands of slain warriors. Rising up, like the echo of an echo, there sounded a faint voice, well-known and well-loved by each of them. And it sang so bitterly and yet so sweetly that surely the angels in heaven wept to hear it. The warriors followed the haunting song to where the head of Donn Bó lay hidden among the reeds. The champion of Munster knelt to pick it up, but the head said, "Nay. Touch me not. Tonight, for the last time, I offer the gift of story and song for our lord Fergal, the King of Erin."

Through his tears, the Munster man replied, "And will you not keep your promise of yesternight, brave Donn Bó? Your comrades have sent us to find you, for they too would hear your tales one last time."

The bloody head of the minstrel replied, "When my tale is told out, when my song here is sung, if God permits, neither death nor darkness shall prevent me. I shall fulfill my promise to the warriors of Erin."

Among the bloodied rushes, they listened to Donn Bó's feeble voice as it told one last king's story, both a song of praise and lament for their fallen chief. When the head at last fell silent, the champion of Munster picked it up and gently bore it on his cloak to where the other warriors awaited. They stopped their feasting and cried, "What have you brought us from the battlefield?"

"I have brought you the head of Donn Bó."

All present fell to their knees and cried, "Oh, most beautiful minstrel, the best in all of Erin, for the love of God, make music. Give us a story to remember this night by, a story that we shall carry forever in our hearts."

The head of Donn Bó turned his face from them and raised his sweet voice in quiet melody. His story was so sad and piteous that the hosts, those hardened warriors, wept like children. In the soft faint voice, they heard once again the clash of steel, the soft ragged sigh of the fallen warrior, the drop of an old woman's tear, and the last beat of a hero's heart. When the teller's tale was told out, he fell silent and his head was taken to join his body. Donn Bó was laid to rest.

Though castles are sacked in war, though chieftains and heroes are scattered and slain, though the heart of the storyteller beats no more, his stories shall live on forever.

"Words are spoken with shells,
and it is left for the intelligence to crack them."
—Mossi folk saying (African)

The Sage's Gift

[MIDDLE EAST]

LONG AGO, IN THE CITY OF BAGHDAD there was a caliph, which is a kind of king. One day a son was born to him. It was his firstborn. In celebration, he ordered a feast to be held. To the feast he invited all the great and well-known people in the land.

On the day of the feast all the guests arrived, each bringing a gift for the child. There were gifts of gold, rare jewels, rich tapestries, carved marble. Everyone brought a gift—except one young sage called Meheled Abi. He came empty-handed. The caliph, taking offense, ordered the guards to seize Meheled Abi. Roughly, the guards dragged the young sage before the caliph, who demanded, "Why do you come without a gift?"

The young sage shrugged and answered, "These others, they bring visible riches; they bring gold, jewels, carpets. But my gift is an invisible wealth. It is this. Each day, when the child is old enough to hear, I will come to the palace and tell him stories. When he is grown, he will be wise and compassionate."

Meheled Abi did as he promised. Each day he came to the palace and the young boy grew up hearing stories. After many years, the old caliph died and the young boy, now grown, succeeded his father. Just as Meheled Abi had promised, the new caliph was wise and compassionate, more so than any ruler before him. And when *he* died, at his request a tomb was erected in the heart of the city with these words inscribed in stone:

If I am wise,
it is because of the seed sown by the tales.

"And this our life, exempt from public haunt,
Finds tongues in trees, books in the running brooks,
Sermons in stones, and good in every thing."
—William Shakespeare
As You Like It (II, i)

The Princes Who Were Blockheads

[INDIA]

ONCE THERE WAS A WISE AND VIRTUOUS KING who had three sons, but they were all blockheads. They not only knew nothing, and were proud of it, but if anyone tried to teach them anything they closed their ears and their minds and sat there as dumb as chunks of wood. Their father was in despair. At last he called his counselors together, and told them the grief of his heart. "What am I to do?" he cried. "What am I to do?"

When the counselors suggested the usual dry-as-dust methods of education, the king groaned and cried, "I tried that long ago!"

At last a counselor asked, "Why not trust them to Vishnusharma, the venerable sage? It is said that he is so full of wisdom that he can make even the greatest truths clear to the mind of a child."

So the old man was summoned from his hermitage in the forest, and the king said, "I pray you, O Vishnusharma, waken the sleeping minds of my three sons. Do this and I will reward you with a hundred tracts of land."

The sage replied, "I have no desire for land, but in six months I will waken the sleeping minds of your three sons." At these words the heart of the king was made glad, and he told Vishnusharma to teach his sons in any way he chose.

Thus it came about that the three princes who were blockheads, and proud of it, never suspected that the sage who made his home in a quiet corner of the palace garden was brought there as a teacher. And as the old man went about his simple life they watched, and wondered about him.

One day the youngest prince asked the sage if there were lions and tigers near his hermitage in the forest. The old man replied that there were, and quite by accident it seemed, he rambled off into a story about a lion. The princes listened with their ears and their minds wide open, and sat there as alert as three cats ready to spring at a mouse, for the lazy rascals liked to be entertained, and they never suspected that they could be taught anything in a story.

Now the first story ended in such a way that it hooked into another like a link in a chain, and the princes leaned forward and cried, "How is that? How is that?"

So the sage told the second story, and the three princes made him promise to go on the next day. The old man chose stories full of laughter, common sense, and wisdom. He sprinkled them generously with many a wise saying from the literature and sacred writings of India. And when the first chain of stories ended, the princes rocked their heads with pleasure and cried, "That was just right! That was just right!" They begged and begged him to tell the whole chain of stories again and again, until they knew them all by heart.

The sage began on another chain of stories, and at the end of six months, those princes who were blockheads, and proud of it, knew every word of five chains of stories, and many a wise saying from the literature and sacred writings. And their ears and their minds were permanently wide open, and they were as alert as three cats ready to spring at a mouse. So the delighted king found them well-fitted to begin to take an active part in ruling his kingdom.

The stories told to the three princes are in the *Panchatantra,* or *Five Books,* which has been translated into many languages so that those who wish to find an easy road to wisdom may read them for themselves.

"A grief shared by many is half a grief.
A joy shared is twice a joy."
—Vietnamese folk saying

Tongue Meat

[SWAHILI (EAST AFRICA)]

THERE WAS ONCE A SULTAN who was both rich and powerful. Yet he had a problem that all his wealth and connection could not overcome. His beloved wife had been fat and healthy when they were first married. But now that they had been married for some years, she had begun to change. His wife took less and less interest in the world around her, and with each passing day she grew more lean and listless.

The sultan ordered his cooks to prepare fine feasts for her, but she had no appetite and refused to eat. He brought in the best physicians in all the land, but they could not cure her. The sultan's chief physician warned him, "We can do no more, Your Highness. We cannot discover the cause of your wife's malady, but if she does not put some meat on her bones, she will not live to see another year."

Messengers were sent throughout the land in search of a cure. One of them returned with news of interest to report.

"Did you find medicine to cure my wife?" demanded the sultan.

"Not exactly, Your Highness, but living in this very city, I came upon a poor man . . ."

"Yes, yes," said the sultan impatiently, "and what is so extraordinary about that?"

"As poor as he is, his wife is as fat and healthy and happy as any woman I have ever seen."

"Send for this man at once!" commanded the sultan.

When the poor man arrived at the palace, he was brought before the sultan for questioning. "Tell me," ordered the sultan, "what is your secret? How is it that a poor man's wife comes to be so fat and healthy, when the wife of a sultan is so gaunt and thin?"

"It is very simple," replied the poor man. "Each night when I come home, I feed her a portion of tongue meat."

The poor man was dismissed and at once the sultan summoned his chief cook. "I have discovered that it is meat of the tongue that will cure my wife. I decree that no animal in this city shall be slaughtered, but that its tongue shall be sent up to the palace for you to prepare for my wife."

So butchers kept the palace supplied and the sultan's cooks prepared the tongue in every imaginable way. The sultan's wife was forced to eat fried tongue, baked tongue, candied, smoked, and roasted tongue three times a day. Yet still she grew thinner and weaker by the hour.

The sultan was desperate. Once again he sent for the poor man and said, "It is clear that my wife will die unless something is done. Perhaps you have some secret recipe, perhaps it is magic. I do not know and I do not care. I have decided that the only way to save her is for us to switch wives. You will bring your wife to live here in the palace and I shall send my wife home with you. Then we shall see what we shall see."

"As you wish," said the poor man.

So the sultan's wife was sent to live in the shabby house of the poor man and the poor man's wife made her new home in the grand palace of the sultan. Weeks went by and the sultan heard no word, good or bad, from either his wife or the poor man. He missed his wife terribly and, after several more weeks, he sent for her. To his shock and dismay, his wife refused to come. The sultan immediately called for his litter and went himself to fetch her. When he arrived and saw with his own eyes the humble little hut of the poor man, he feared that he had sent his wife here to starve to death.

But she had not starved. In fact, when he demanded to see his wife, he hardly recognized her, for she had grown sleek and fat and beautiful. Her skin glowed and her eyes sparkled. "My wife," cried the sultan, "what has this man done to effect such a miracle?"

She smiled and replied, "Every night he comes home to me and he tells me stories that make me laugh until I cry. He sings me songs and amuses me. Even during the day, when he is gone, all I have to do is think of the funny stories that he told the night before and I find myself smiling or even laughing aloud to myself. I have never been so happy."

At first the sultan frowned, for now he understood what the poor man had meant by "tongue meat." But then he looked at his wife and remembered his love for her. At last he asked her, "And if I should learn to prepare and serve you such fare, wife, then would you come home with me?"

She looked at her husband, smiled, and gave him her hand.

After that, storytellers and musicians throughout the land knew that they would find a warm welcome at the sultan's palace. They came from far and wide to tell their stories and to learn new ones as well, for in the fullness of time the sultan too learned to serve up a fine dish of tongue meat.

"We shall exist as long as
our stories are moist with our breath."
—Navaho saying

Hoichi

[JAPAN]

ONCE LONG AGO IN A SMALL COASTAL VILLAGE there lived a blind man named Hoichi. He was famous for his skill at playing the *biwa*, a four-stringed lute, but even more so for his recitation of stories and poetry. Of all the stories Hoichi told, it was the story of the last great battle between the Heike and the Genji clans that people came to hear. At the Battle of Dan-no-ura, fought in the waves off the nearby shore some seven hundred years before, the Genji clan destroyed the Heike clan. Visitors often came to the cemetery where the infant emperor of the Heike and all his followers were buried, and to hear Hoichi sing the Battle of Dan-no-ura.

Years before, Hoichi had been taken in by the priest at the Amidaji temple, for the old priest was so fond of music and poetry and storytelling that he asked nothing more of Hoichi than to listen to him play his *biwa* and recite a story each night. It was a very good arrangement for both of them.

One night the old priest and his acolyte were called away. It was a warm evening so Hoichi waited for the priest's return on the cool verandah of the temple and passed the time by singing to himself the story of the Battle of Dan-no-ura. It was midnight when Hoichi heard the sound of footsteps approaching. At first he thought that the priest was returning at last, but from the heavy tread and the clink of armor, Hoichi realized that his visitor must be a samurai warrior. Then he heard a deep voice calling gruffly from below the verandah. "Hoichi," it said. "Hoichi."

"I am here," replied Hoichi. "But I am blind. Please tell me who you are and what you wish of me."

"My lord has come to visit the site of the Battle of Dan-no-ura and has heard of your skill in reciting the story," said the stranger. "He has commanded me to escort you to him. Bring your *biwa* and I shall take you to where my lord and his noble followers await."

Before Hoichi could reply, he felt his wrist grasped in an iron grip. The order of a samurai was not to be taken lightly, so Hoichi nervously shuffled on his sandals and took up his *biwa* to go with the stranger.

They had not gone far when Hoichi heard the samurai calling for a gate to be opened. He heard the unbarring of iron. Then came the shuffling sound of many feet, the whispering of voices. Hoichi was ordered to remove his sandals and a woman then took his hand. He listened to the murmur of voices and the rustle of silk as he felt himself guided to the center of a vast apartment, where a great company was assembled. Once the blind man was seated upon a cushion, the company fell silent. "Now you must recite to us the history of the Heike clan," the woman told him.

"To tell such a story would require many nights," said Hoichi. "Is there some portion of the story which would find the most favor with you?"

"Sing to us the Battle of Dan-no-ura," she replied.

Hoichi's skill made the strings of the *biwa* sound like the straining of oars and the rushing of ships. Behind the notes of the *biwa* the company could almost hear the shouting of men, the whirring of arrows, the crash of cold steel upon helmed head. Hoichi felt the room take up the thrill of battle and when he came to the end, where the helpless women and children of the Heike clan were slaughtered and the emperor's mother made her courageous death-leap into the sea with the imperial infant in her arms, the company wept.

Gradually the sounds of sorrow died away and in the stillness that followed, the woman said to Hoichi, "Surely in all the realm there is no one to equal your skill as a storyteller. My lord commands you to perform before him for the next six nights. The samurai will come for you at the temple at this same hour tomorrow. But my lord commands that you speak to no one of your visit." Hoichi was then guided back to the temple by the same hard grip of the samurai.

It was almost dawn, but his absence had not been noticed, for the priest, who had returned at a very late hour, assumed him to be asleep. Hoichi said nothing of his strange visit and the next evening the samurai came and took Hoichi to play before the fine company. But that night Hoichi's absence was noticed. In the morning, the old priest summoned him and said, "I was very anxious for you last night, my friend. To go out, blind and alone, so late at night is dangerous. In the future, if you wish to go out, please allow me to send a servant to guide you. What took you away from the temple at such an hour?"

"I had some private business to attend to," explained Hoichi.

But the old priest suspected that there was more to the matter than that. He instructed his servants to keep a secret watch upon Hoichi and to follow him if he should leave the temple grounds. But that night it was dark and rainy and the blind man was accustomed to the darkness. When he left the temple, Hoichi moved so quickly that the others soon lost sight of him. The priest's servants hurried through the village streets making inquiries, but no one in the district had seen the blind storyteller. It was on their return to the temple that they were startled to hear the sounds of Hoichi's *biwa*.

They quickly extinguished their lanterns and crept silently toward the sound. Chills ran up their spines when they realized that it was coming from the temple cemetery, where the Heike clan had been buried after the Battle of Dan-no-ura. It was there that they discovered Hoichi, sitting alone beside the tomb of the long dead Heike emperor. As the storyteller chanted the Battle of Dan-no-ura, everywhere about him there were eerie, flickering flames, burning like candles and growing in brightness with each word.

"Hoichi-san!" called the men, "Hoichi!" But the blind man did not seem to hear. "Hoichi!" they called again more insistently. At last the servants braved the strange lights to take the storyteller by the arm and shout into his ear, "Hoichi-san, you are bewitched!"

"How dare you!" cried the blind man. "To interrupt me when I am playing for such a noble company!"

"Hoichi, you are playing for the dead!"

The servants refused to argue, but took Hoichi by force back to the temple. Hoichi was brought before the old priest, who was finally able to make the storyteller understand his danger. "My friend, by your skill, you have conjured up the dead. Each night you give them more life from your art. By obeying them even once, you have put yourself in their power!"

Hoichi recalled the stories told about the ghosts of the Heike dead. He remembered then that the Amidaji temple had been built to appease those restless spirits, for they were said to haunt the seashore where they had died so violently seven hundred years before. On dark nights the demon flames were said to flit above the waves, and whenever the winds were up, the clamor of battle was said to be heard along that dismal shore. Fishermen told stories of bitter ghosts who would try to sink passing ships or pull swimmers down beneath the waves. And now . . .

"What have I done?" cried Hoichi in alarm.

"We must do what we can to free you from their power," said the old priest, "and hope that we are not too late."

Before sunset the next day, the priest and his acolyte began their rites. They stripped Hoichi and wrote holy texts and prayers all over his body. With their brushes, they traced his chest, his back, his head and face, his limbs and hands and feet. When they were done, they laid him on the verandah. "Be very silent and very still," the priest warned him, "and whatever happens, do not cry out. If you do everything I tell you to do, perhaps you will be freed of the dead."

Then they left him and went to pray for his safety. Hoichi, his *biwa* beside him on the verandah, lay as still as death. For hours he stayed there, hardly daring to breathe. It was just midnight when he heard the heavy footsteps of the samurai approach and the deep dreaded voice call out, "Hoichi. My lord awaits you. Hoichi!"

Hoichi held very still and hoped that the pounding of his heart would not give him away.

"Where is the priest?" growled the ghost savagely. Hoichi felt the verandah sag beneath the weight of the dead samurai. The footsteps walked up and down and then stopped directly beside him. Hoichi was terrified, but he made no sound.

"Ahhh!" said the samurai. "Here is the *biwa*, but where is the player? I see no man; only two ears. Well, they are better than nothing. I will take them back to my lord." Hoichi kept his silence, though the pain could hardly be borne as he felt his ears gripped by fingers of iron and torn off by the samurai. From either side of his head, Hoichi felt the warm trickling of blood running down his cheeks. But even after the sound of the samurai's footfalls receded into the darkness, Hoichi dared not stir.

The next morning the priest hurried out to the verandah and found Hoichi, free of ghosts—and ears. The old priest frowned and shook his head. "Forgive me, old friend," he apologized. "The holy writings that my acolyte and I painted on your body made you invisible to the ghosts," he explained, "but it is very difficult to write on ears."

Hoichi recovered from his wounds and, as the story of his adventure spread throughout the land, he became even more famous for his skill as a storyteller and player of the *biwa*. But from that time on, he was known only as "Hoichi the Earless." And he never told the story of the Battle of Dan-no-ura again.

"When the heart overflows,
it comes out through the mouth."
—Ethiopian folk saying

Tell It to the Walls

[TAMIL (INDIA)]

A POOR WIDOW LIVED WITH HER TWO SONS and two daughters-in-law. All four of them scolded and ill-treated her all day. She had no one to whom she could turn and tell her woes. As she kept her woes to herself, she grew fatter and fatter. Her sons and daughters-in-law now found *that* a matter for ridicule. They mocked at her for growing fatter by the day and asked her to eat less.

One day, when everyone in the house had gone out somewhere, she wandered away from home in sheer misery and found herself walking outside town. There she saw a deserted old house. It was in ruins and had no roof. She went in and suddenly felt lonelier and more miserable than ever; she found she couldn't bear to keep her miseries to herself any longer. She had to tell someone.

So she told all her tales of grievance against her first son to the wall in front of her. As she finished, the wall collapsed under the weight of her woes and crashed to the ground in a heap. Her body grew lighter as well.

Then she turned to the second wall and told it all her grievances against her first son's wife. Down came that wall, and she grew lighter still. She brought down the third wall with her tales against her second son, and the remaining fourth wall, too, with her complaints against her second daughter-in-law.

Standing in the ruins, with bricks and rubble all around her, she felt lighter in mood and lighter in body as well. She looked at herself and found she had actually lost all the weight she had gained in her wretchedness.

Then she went home.

"A wise man hears one word and understands two."
—Yiddish folk saying

Wisdom

[INDIA]

MANY HUNDREDS OF YEARS AGO, a young king desired wisdom. He called upon his philosopher, mathematician, physician, historian, storyteller and fool, and challenged them to research and write a complete history of humankind.

"Leave out nothing of significance," he explained.

After thirty years of painstaking effort, the advisors presented the now middle-aged king a vast library filled with leather-clad volumes. It contained the fruits of their labors.

The ruler was as exasperated as he was pleased.

"I'm far too busy to read so many books," he explained. "Thus, I offer a second challenge. Distill all that you've learned into a single book."

Another twenty years were required to accomplish the task. At last, the thick volume, containing a condensed version of human knowledge throughout time, was presented to the now elderly and failing king.

"I'm too old and my eyes too weak to read such a heavy tome," he said. "My third challenge is for the storyteller. Tell me the story of this book. Give me the wisdom of humankind before I take my final breath."

The storyteller agreed. He paused, and thought. Finally he said, "They were born. They lived. They knew sorrow. They knew joy. They died. We learn."

"A story, a story
Let it come.
Let it go."
—Traditional West African opening

How All Stories Came to Be Known as Spider Stories

[ASHANTI (WEST AFRICA)]

LONG, LONG AGO ALL STORIES BELONGED TO NYANKONPON, the Sky God. Then Kwaku Anansi, the Spider Man, spun a web up to the sky. Anansi told the Sky God that he wanted to buy his stories. The Sky God laughed and said, "How can a small man like you buy my stories when the richest and most powerful men have already tried and failed?"

"What is the price?" asked Anansi.

"Nothing less than Onini the Python, Osebo the Leopard, Mmboro the Hornet, and Mmoatia the Tree Spirit," replied the Sky God.

"I shall gladly pay the price and will throw in my old mother as well," said Anansi proudly.

But as Anansi climbed back down to earth, he did not know how he would fulfill the Sky God's demands. He went to consult his wife, Aso. She said to her husband, "What you do is cut a long pole and some strong vine-creepers. Take them to the stream . . ."

"Enough," cried Anansi. "I understand."

Anansi cut a long pole and some vine-creepers. Then he went down to the stream where Onini the Python made his home. As he was going along, Anansi said aloud, "Yes, he is. No, he's not. Yes, he is. No, he's not."

Onini the Python overheard Anansi talking to himself and called, "What is this all about, Anansi?"

"I am having an argument with my wife," replied Anansi. "She says that my pole is longer and stronger than you are, but I say that you are longer and stronger than my pole."

"Of course I am longer and stronger and I will prove it!" said the indignant python. "Come and measure me."

Anansi set the long pole on the ground and told Onini, "Stretch yourself out beside my pole then."

Onini slithered over to the pole and stretched himself out beside it.

"Stretch yourself out a little more," urged Anansi. So Onini stretched himself out even farther.

"Well?" asked the python.

"It is difficult to say," said Anansi with a frown. "When you stretch at the front, the back end slips. When you stretch yourself out at the back, the front end slips. I had better tie you down so that we can be certain." With that, Anansi used the vine-creepers to tie the enormous snake to the pole.

"What do you think, Anansi?" asked Onini.

"I think you are a fool," replied the Spider Man. "Now prepare to meet the Sky God, for I am taking you to Nyankonpon in exchange for his stories."

Anansi spun a web around the angry python and hung him up in a tree. Then he went to Aso and said, "Now I must capture Osebo the Leopard."

His wife said, "What you do is dig a hole . . ."

"Enough," cried Anansi. "I understand."

Anansi hurried off in search of leopard tracks. When he found them, he dug a deep hole, covered it over, and then he settled down to wait for Osebo. It wasn't long before Osebo came walking along the path and fell into the hole. She roared and struggled to get out of that hole, but it was too deep. Anansi went to the edge of the hole and looked down. "What are you doing in that hole, Osebo?" he asked.

"What does it matter?" she growled. "Let me out."

"That I cannot do," said Anansi, "for you would surely eat me."

"I would not return evil for good."

"So that I can be certain you will not eat me, you must first let me bind your paws."

"Very well," grumbled Osebo, who then lifted her paws high enough for Anansi to bind them with a vine-creeper. Once the leopard was secured, Anansi pulled her up out of the hole, but he did not untie her.

"Let me go!" roared the leopard. "What do you think you are doing?"

"I think I am taking you to the Sky God in exchange for his stories," said Anansi. With that, he carried her to the tree where Onini the Python was waiting. Anansi then spun a web around Osebo the Leopard and left her hanging in the tree as well.

Anansi went back to Aso and said, "Now I must obtain Mmboro the Hornet."

His wife said, "What you do is find a gourd and fill it with water . . ."

"Enough," cried Anansi. "I understand."

Anansi hurried off to find a gourd, which he filled with water. He cut a big plantain leaf and carried both the gourd and the leaf to the tree where a nest of hornets hung. Anansi sprinkled some of the water on himself and the rest of the water he sprinkled over the nest. Then he held the plantain leaf above his head as though to protect himself from the rain. "It is raining," cried Anansi. "Hurry into my gourd so that you will not get wet!"

The hornets swarmed into the gourd which Anansi held up for

them. When the last hornet had flown into his gourd, Anansi plugged the opening with a ball of grass.

"Thank you, thank you," said the hornets to Anansi.

"No," replied the Spider Man. "Thank *you*, for I am going to give you to the Sky God in exchange for his stories."

Anansi spun a web about the gourd and hung it in the tree with the python and the leopard. Then he went to Aso and said, "Now I have only to get Mmoatia, the Tree Spirit."

His wife said, "What you do is carve a wooden doll . . ."

"Enough," cried Anansi. "I understand."

Anansi went to the tree where the fairies loved to play. There he carved a little wooden doll holding a bowl. He covered the doll with sticky tree sap, and then filled her bowl with pounded yams. Last of all, Anansi tied one end of a vine-creeper around the little doll's neck. Holding the other end of the vine, he went to hide in the bushes nearby. Anansi waited until Mmoatia the Tree Spirit came dancing along. When she saw the little doll holding the bowl of yams, she said, "Mmmm, little one, may I have some of your yams?"

Anansi pulled on his end of the vine and the doll appeared to nod her head in reply.

"Good," said Mmoatia, and she ate all the yams in the doll's bowl. Then, licking her fingers, she said, "Thank you, little one."

The Tree Spirit waited for a reply, but of course the wooden doll said nothing.

"Do you not answer me when I thank you?"

Still the doll made no reply.

"Answer me when I speak to you or I'll slap your crying place!" said the angry fairy.

When the doll gave no answer, Mmoatia slapped its cheek. The little fairy's hand stuck fast in the sticky sap. "Let go of my hand or I'll slap you again," she cried. With that, she slapped the doll again on its other cheek. That hand was then stuck fast as well. The tree spirit tried to push the doll away with her foot, but her foot was then caught in the sap. She used her other foot, but then that too was caught.

Anansi stepped out of hiding and said, "Prepare to meet the Sky God, Mmoatia, for I am going to exchange you for his stories."

Anansi spun a web around Mmoatia, then carried the little fairy over his shoulder as he went home to fetch his old mother. "Come, Mother," Anansi told her, "for I have promised you to Nyankonpon in exchange for his stories."

Anansi carried Mmoatia the Tree Spirit and led his old mother back to the tree where he had left Onini the Python, Osebo the Leopard, and Mmboro the Hornet hanging. He carried his captives up the web and into the sky and set them at the feet of the Sky God.

"O, Nyankonpon," said the Spider Man, "here is the price you asked for your stories: Onini the Python, Osebo the Leopard, Mmboro the Hornet, Mmoatia the Tree Spirit, and I have thrown in my old mother as well, just as I promised."

"What my hand has touched, my hand has touched," said Nyankonpon. The Sky God called all his helpers together and announced, "Many great men have tried to buy my stories, but they have failed. Kwaku Anansi has paid me the price I asked for my stories. Sing his praise. From this day and going on forever, my stories belong to Anansi and shall be called 'Spider Stories.' "

Anansi thanked the Sky God and climbed back down to earth with his prize. That was a very long time ago. Since that day, the stories have scattered to all corners of the world. People everywhere still tell Anansi's stories, including this one.

If my story be sweet, if it is not sweet,
take some elsewhere and let some come back to me.

"Fair speech turns elephants away from the garden path."
—Swahili folk saying

Why People Tell Tales

[ROMANIA]

THERE WERE ONCE THREE MEN WHO WERE TRAVELING TOGETHER. It was late in the year and the snow lay thick on the ground. As evening drew near, the wind blew up a gale and fresh snow began to fall. The travelers watched for a house or an inn where they might find shelter. At last they saw a light shining in the distance. They followed it to a little cottage and knocked on the door. An old woman came to the door and opened it a crack.

"Please let us in out of this storm," they pleaded. "We'll be glad to pay for a bit of bread and a place by your fire."

"I'll have a story from each of you and welcome," she said, "but if you've no story to tell, then be off with you."

"Gladly!" said the first man.

"Gladly!" said the second.

The third man said nothing.

The three companions went inside and, while her guests settled themselves by the blazing fire, the old woman served a steaming bowl of porridge to each of them. She gave each man a blanket to wrap up in and, while she built up the fire, they took off their shoes and warmed toes grown numb with the cold. Then the old woman sat down in a chair beside the fire and said, "I've kept my part of the bargain. Now you keep yours."

The first of the three men told a funny story about the antics of two rogues named Pacala and Tandala. After the old woman had caught her breath from laughing so hard, she said to the storyteller, "I thank you kindly. May God reward you."

Then the second traveler took his turn. He told a beautiful story about good Prince Stephen. The old woman wiped a tear from her eye and said to the storyteller, "I thank you kindly. May God reward you."

All eyes turned expectantly toward the third traveler, but he said nothing. So the old woman said, "And what story will you tell tonight?"

He shrugged. "I don't know any stories."

"Not even a short story?"

"I told you I haven't a story in my head," he snapped.

"Didn't your grandmother ever take you up on her knee and tell you a story?"

"I don't remember it if she did," he replied.

"Surely something has happened to you in your life. Tell us about that," urged his hostess.

"Look here," said the traveler. "I told you before I was willing to pay for my bread. Why all this fuss over a silly story?"

"Well, if that's all you have to say, get out of my house!" cried the old woman. She didn't even give him the time to put on his shoes. In a trice, she took up her straw broom, drove him out the door, and bolted it behind him. Before he knew what had happened, the man with no story was barefoot and shivering outside her house in the cold dark night.

He glanced up the road and saw a light in the distance. Teeth chattering, boots in hand, he ran through the snow toward the light as fast as his frozen feet would carry him. He went up to the window of the house and peeked in, thinking to knock on the windowpane.

But his hand froze in mid-air, not from the cold, but from sheer terror. What did he see? A man and a woman were asleep in bed. And while they slept, a huge snake coiled its tail around the big beam overhead and hung down over the sleeping couple. Its jaws were wide open and from its fangs drops of poison dripped into the open mouths of its victims.

The poor traveler screamed and took to his heels. He went tripping and stumbling through the frozen darkness toward the next lighted house. Breathless from fear and exertion, he ran up to the window and peeked inside. His heart slammed against his chest and he nearly fainted from fright at the sight that met his eyes. What did he see? There was a man lying in bed with a big axe buried in his chest.

The traveler shrieked and fled from the house, heedless of wind and weather, his only thought to escape. Then up ahead he saw another light. The cold was now more than he could bear, so he followed the bright light up a hill to a house. But then he stopped dead in his tracks, halted by the strangest sight he had ever seen in his life. What did he see? There were three brilliant flames racing around and around the house, lighting up the sky and reflecting off the snow. Even if the traveler had been of a mind to peek into the window, he could not have gone near the house, let alone gone inside.

The poor man knew that if he didn't find shelter soon, he would surely freeze to death. There was nothing for it, but to go back to the house of the old woman. He pounded on her door and cried, "Let me in! Let me in! I'm the man who has a story to tell!"

The door swung open and the dazed and bedraggled man was soon kneeling before a blazing fire. When he had caught his breath, he looked up at the old woman and said, "Is it a story you want?" He then began to tell the old woman and his two companions all that had befallen him after he had been thrown out into the night. When he had finished, the old woman said, "I thank you kindly for your story. May God reward you.

"Now it is your turn to listen, and listen carefully," she warned.

"In the first house you went to, that wasn't a snake at all, but a belt. Instead of putting his belt away at night, the foolish man left it hanging on the beam. You must never leave your belt on a beam when you go to bed, but be sure to put it away.

"In the second house you went to, that wasn't an axe planted in the man's chest, but a warning from the axe. If you were to go back to his house, you would find that the foolish man must have been chopping wood and left his axe outside in the chopping block, instead of storing it safely away in the shed."

"But what about the third house?" asked the man. "That was the strangest of all."

"Ah, the third house, where you saw the three fiery flames," said the old woman. "That was a house where three people were sleeping after each one had told a story. Each story had turned into a fiery flame and was protecting the house so that no foe could come near it.

"And that," concluded the old woman, "is why you are doing a good deed when you give the gift of a story to your host."

The traveler never forgot the old woman's words. From that time on, he was never without a story. Wherever his travels took him, wherever he made his bed that night, he was sure to ask for a tale and to tell one himself before closing his eyes. Of course, the story he told was always the same one, about the time he had been a man with no story.

"From your lips to God's ears."
—Yiddish folk saying

Lighting the Fire

[HASIDIC (JEWISH)]

WHENEVER THE GREAT RABBI BAL SHEM TOV SAW DANGER threatening the Jews, he would make a journey to a sacred place in the heart of the forest. There he would light a fire according to ancient ritual, and say a special prayer. God would hear his plea for his people, a miracle would occur, and the crisis would be averted.

Many peaceful and prosperous years passed. Eventually the Rabbi Bal Shem Tov died and was succeeded by a disciple who was both good and holy. By the time misfortune again threatened the Jews, this rabbi was an old, old man. He journeyed to the sacred spot in the forest, but he found that he could no longer remember the ritual manner in which to light the fire. Yet the words to the special prayer were engraved in his heart. He looked up to the heavens and called, "Oh, Lord of the Universe, I do not remember how to light the fire, but I offer you the prescribed prayer and this must be sufficient." God heard his prayer, a miracle occurred, and the Jews were saved.

The good fortune of the people continued. By the time danger once again threatened the community, the new rabbi had never learned the special words of prayer and of course the sacred fire-lighting ritual had long since been forgotten. But he found his way to the special place deep in the heart of the forest. The rabbi lifted his eyes to heaven and spoke. "Lord of the Universe, I do not know how to light the fire. I cannot say the sacred prayer. But I have come here to this, your sacred place, to ask you to intercede on behalf of your people, and this must be sufficient." It was. A miracle occurred, and once again the Jews were saved.

Generations went by. When misfortune threatened the Jews once more, it fell upon their rabbi to go to God on behalf of his people. Though the rabbi was a good man, he could not light the fire in the ritual manner, he could not say the prescribed prayer, and even the sacred place in the forest had long been forgotten. From his own chair, his head in his hands, the rabbi spoke to God. "Lord of the Universe, I cannot light the fire. I cannot say the prayer. I cannot even find your sacred place in the forest. All I can do is tell the story, and this must be sufficient." And it was, for God was listening. He sent a miracle, and once again the Jews were saved.

So it is to this day. The sacred place is in our thoughts, the sacred fire is in our hearts, and if we tell the story, God will listen.

"I jumped in the saddle and rode away
To tell you the stories you've heard today.
I jumped on a spoon and away I flew
And you've heard all my stories, so God bless you.
I jumped on a spindle and away I spun
And God bless me! My stories are done."
—Romanian folk saying

Sources and Variants

1. "The Golden Lamb" is retold by Naomi Baltuck and is adapted with permission of Atheneum Books for Young Readers, an imprint of Simon & Schuster Children's Publishing Division from *Palace in Bagdad: Seven Tales from Arabia* by Jean Russell Larson. Text copyright © Jean Russell Larson. With special thanks to the author.

2. "The Dragon King's Feast" is retold by Naomi Baltuck. It is adapted from two Chinese stories, both of which poke good-natured fun at boasters. Short written versions of this story can by found in *Wit and Humor of Old Cathay*, translated by Jon Kowallis (San Francisco: Chinese Literature Press, 1984), p. 42 and in *Quips from a Chinese Jest-book*, by Herbert A. Giles (Shanghai: Kelly and Walsh, 1925), pp. 145–46.

3. "The Woodcutter's Daughter" from *The Stories of the Steppes: Kazakh Folktales*, p. 73, is retold by Mary Lou Masey. Copyright © 1968 by Mary Lou Masey. Reprinted by permission of David McKay Co., a division of Random House, Inc. Thanks also to Sharon Creeden for introducing me to this tale.

4. "Cutting a Story Down to Size" is retold by Naomi Baltuck. Brief variants of this tale may be found in *A World of Nonsense* by Carl Withers (New York: Holt, Rinehart and Winston, 1968), p. 29, and in *Flatlanders and Ridgerunners* by James York Glimm (Pittsburgh: University of Pittsburgh Press, 1983), p. 48.

5. "The Most Noble Story" is retold by Naomi Baltuck. Variants of this tale may be found as "Los Tres Hijos" by Howard T. Wheeler in *Tales from Jalisco, Mexico* (Philadelphia: American Folklore Society, 1943) and as "The Noblest Deed" by Grant Lyons in *Tales People Tell in Mexico* (New York: Julian Messner, 1972), p. 54.

6. "Ali the Persian" is retold by Naomi Baltuck. It is adapted from Richard F. Burton's "Tale of Ali the Persian" in *The Book of the Thousand Nights and a Night* (Benares: Kamashastra Society, 1885–88). Special thanks to my sister Deborah Baltuck for introducing me to this tale.

7. "The Four Ne'er-do-wells" is adapted from "The Four Ne'er-do-wells" in *Jewish Folktales*, by Pinhas Sadeh, p. 320. Copyright © 1989 by Doubleday, a division of Bantam Doubleday Dell Publishing Group, Inc. Used by permission of Doubleday, a division of Bantam Doubleday Dell Publishing Group, Inc. There is a variant of this story from the Middle East where Mullah Nasruddin is the thief making excuses.

8. "The Story Spirits" is retold by Naomi Baltuck. There are many versions of this story, mostly of Korean origin, circulating throughout the storytelling community, although I have come across Cambodian and Kazakh versions as well. Two variants of this tale are "The Story Bag" by Kim So-Un in *The Story Bag: A Collection of Korean Folk Tales* (Rutland, Vt: Charles E. Tuttle Co., 1955), p. 3 and "The Story Spirits," retold by Amabel Williams-Ellis in *Round the World Fairy Tales* (New York: Frederick Warne & Co., 1963), p. 279.

9. "The Humbled Storyteller" is retold by Naomi Baltuck. It is adapted from a Russian variant, "Once There Was and Once There Was Not," by Lee Wyndham, which can be found in *Tales the People Tell in Russia* (New York: Julian Messner, 1970), p. 62. I have found similar stories from Japan, Portugal, and Thailand.

10. "The Storyteller at Fault" is retold by Naomi Baltuck. It is adapted from the story collected by Joseph Jacobs in *Celtic Fairy Tales* (London: David Nutt, 1892), p. 131.

11. "Now, That's a Story!" is retold by Naomi Baltuck. It is adapted from "That's Not True!" in *Old Hungarian Fairy Tales* by Baroness Orczy (London: Dean, 1895). Other variants of this story may be found throughout Europe, Asia, and the Middle East. Several other variants include "Boots Who Made the Princess Say, 'That's a Story,' " (Norwegian) in *East o' the Sun and West o' the Moon*, by Asbjornsen and Moe, p. 48; "The Peasant and the Czar" (Russian) in *Eurasian Folk and Fairy Tales* by Bulatkin, p. 75, and "A Tall Tale" in *Jewish Stories One Generation Tells Another* by Schram, p. 279.

12. "Little Bobtail" is retold by Naomi Baltuck. It is adapted from an Inuit story, "Brave Vuvyltu," which may be found in *Kutkha the Raven: Animal Stories of the North*, by Fainna Solasko (Malysh Publishers, 1981), p. 72. There is a similar story from the Middle East, in which a donkey brags of kicking a lion but confesses that the lion was dead at the time.

13. "A Fair Price for a Story" is retold by Naomi Baltuck. Variants of this tale include "The Firewalkers" by Anne Gittins in *Tales from the South Pacific Islands* (Owings Mills, Md.: Stemmer House, 1977), p. 11; "The Firewalkers of Beqa" by Mary Edith and Joel S. Branham in *Bed the Turtle Softly: Legends of the South Pacific* (Mukilteo,

Wash.: Scott Publications, 1975), p. 135; and "The Firewalkers of Beqa" by A. W. Reed and Inez Hames in *Myths and Legends of Fiji and Rotuma* (Wellington-Auckland-Sydney: A. H. & A. W. Reed, 1967). Special thanks to Margaret Read MacDonald for introducing me to this tale.

14. "A Sackful of Stories" is retold by Naomi Baltuck. There are scores of variants from all over Europe, including Gypsy, Lithuanian, Jewish, and Norwegian versions. Several variants include "Jesper Who Herded the Hares," retold by Andrew Lang in *The Violet Fairy Book* (London: Longmans, Green and Co., 1901), p. 205 and "The King's Hares" by Stith Thompson in *100 Favorite Folktales*, no. 57 (Bloomington: Indiana University Press, 1968).

15. "Truth and Parable" is retold by Naomi Baltuck. There are many oral versions of this tale circulating throughout the storytelling community. A brief written variant may be found in "Naked Truth and Resplendent Parable" by Beatrice Silverman Wienreich in *Yiddish Folktales* (New York: Pantheon, 1977), p. 7.

16. "Conal Crovi" is retold by Naomi Baltuck based on variants including "The Tale of Conal Crovi" by J. F. Campbell in *Popular Tales of the West Highlands,* v. 1 (Edinburgh: Edmonston and Douglas, 1860), p. 128 and "Conall Yellowclaw" by Joseph Jacobs in *Celtic Fairy Tales* (London: David Nutt, 1892), p. 34.

17. "The Gossiping Clams" is adapted from *Ah Mo: Indian Legends from the Northwest*, compiled by Arthur Griffin. Copyright © 1990 by Arthur Griffin. Reprinted by permission of Hancock House Publishers.

18. "The Endless Story" is retold by Naomi Baltuck. This tale has variants from all over Europe, Asia, and North America, including "The Endless Tale" by Ralph Steele Boggs and Mary Gould Davis in *Three Golden Oranges and Other Spanish Folk Tales* (New York: David McKay Co., 1936), p. 84; "The Endless Story" by Ahmed and Zane Zagloul in *The Black Prince and Other Egyptian Folk Tales* (New York: Doubleday, 1971), p. 155; and "The Man with the Long Tales" by Joe Neil MacNeil in *Tales Until Dawn: The World of a Cape Breton Gaelic Story-Teller,* (Kingston and Montreal: McGill-Queen's University Press, 1987), p. 70.

19. "The Silent Princess" is retold by Naomi Baltuck. It is adapted from "The Silent Princess" by Andrew Lang in *The Olive Fairy Book* (London: Longmans, Green and Co., 1907), p. 319. A Jewish version of this story, "The Mute Princess" by Howard Schwartz, can be found in *Elijah's Violin and Other Jewish Fairy Tales*, p. 148.

20. "Backing Up a Story" is retold by Naomi Baltuck. Brief variants of this story may be found in the *China Review*, v. 14, (1885–86), pp. 87–88 and as "Wife Helps Out Her Boastful Husband" in *Gems of Chinese Humor* by Hollington K. Tong, (1957) pp. 67–68.

21. "The Storytelling Stone" is retold by Naomi Baltuck. Several variants are "The Storytelling Stone" by Joseph Bruchac in *Return of the Sun: Native American Tales from the Northeast Woodlands* (1990), p. 35; "The Storytelling Stone" by Jeremiah Curtin in *Seneca Indian Myths* (1923); and "The Talking Stone" by Caroline Cunningham in *The Talking Stone* (1939), p. 3.

22. "The Head of Donn Bó" is retold by Naomi Baltuck. Several variants are "The Talking Head of Donn Bó" by Eleanor Hull in *The Irish Fairy Book* by Alfred Perceval Graves (New York: Greenwich House), p. 243; "Donn Bó" by Arthur C. L. Brown in *The Origin of the Grail Legend* (Cambridge, Mass.: Harvard University Press, 1943), p. 294; and "The Battle of Allen" by Myles Dillon in *The Cycles of the Kings* (London: Oxford University Press, 1946), p. 99. In some versions of this story, when Donn Bó's head rejoins his body, he comes back to life and returns to his mother.

23. "The Sage's Gift" is from *Storytelling: A Creative Teaching Strategy* by Sheila Dailey Carroll. Copyright © 1985 by Sheila Dailey Carroll (Storytime Productions, 1326 E. Broadway, Mt. Pleasant, Michigan 48858). Reprinted by permission of the author.

24. "The Princes Who Were Blockheads" is from *Picture Tales from India* by Berta Metzger (Philadelphia: J.B. Lippincott Co., 1942), p. 63. Special thanks to Sharon Creeden for recommending this tale to me.

25. "Tongue Meat" is retold by Naomi Baltuck. There are many oral versions of this tale circulating throughout the storytelling community. A written variant may be found in *Myths and Legends of the Swahili* by Jan Knappert (London: Heinemann Educational Books, 1970), p. 132.

26. "Hoichi" is retold by Naomi Baltuck. It is adapted from Lafcadio Hearn's "The Story of Mimi-Nashi-Hoichi" in *Kwaidon: Stories and Studies of Strange Things* (Boston: Houghton Mifflin & Co., 1904). There is another story, "Dan'ichi Whose Ears Were Cut Off," by Fanny Magin Mayer in *Ancient Tales in Modern Japan*, in which a novice priest loses his ears to a demon because the priest forgets to write holy texts on his ears.

27. "Tell It to the Walls" is from *Folktales from India* by A. K. Rumanujan, p. 3. Copyright © 1991 by A. K. Rumanujan. Reprinted by permission of Pantheon Books, a division of Random House, Inc. Special thanks to Mary Love May for bringing this story to my attention.

28. "Wisdom" by Pleasant DeSpain is used by permission of the author. Copyright © 1994 Pleasant DeSpain. Pleasant writes, "What is the best source for wisdom? I

asked Muktananda, a guru from the East, this question during my first and only visit with him. I was young, naive, and searching for enlightenment.

"He laughed and said, 'Wisdom isn't found in a book. It's found in living life with open eyes, ears, and heart.'

"Then he told a story about a prince who told his advisors to travel the world in search of wisdom and report back to him.

"This is my version of that tale, some twenty-two years after hearing it. Retaining its essence, I've condensed it considerably over time. Genuine wisdom, I've discovered, doesn't require lengthy explanation."

29. "How Stories Came to Be Known as Spider Stories" is retold by Naomi Baltuck. There are many written variants of this story, including "All Stories Are Anansi's" by Harold Courlander in *The Hat-Shaking Dance and Other Tales from the Gold Coast* (New York: Harcourt, Brace and Co., 1957), p. 3; "How Spider Obtained the Sky-God's Stories" by R. S. Rattray in *Akan-Ashanti Folk Tales* (Oxford: Oxford University Press, 1930), and "The Conceited Spider" by F. H. Lee in *Folk Tales of All Nations* (New York: Tudor Publishing Co., 1930), p. 24.

30. "Why People Tell Stories" is retold by Naomi Baltuck. Adapted from a Romanian folk tale collected by Jean Ure in *Rumanian Folk Tales* (New York: Franklin Watts, Inc., 1960), p. 172; and "Poveste" by A. Vasiliu, in the Romanian journal of folklore *Sezatoarea*, v. 9, no. 8, p. 96. Special thanks to Mihail Ionescu for translating this story from the Romanian into English for me.

31. "Lighting the Fire" is retold by Naomi Baltuck. I have heard many oral versions of this story, but several written variants may be found, including "A Hasidic Tale" by John Harrell in *A Storyteller's Treasury*, p. 53, and "A Hasidic Tale" by Peninnah Schram in *Jewish Stories One Generation Tells Another* (Northvale, N.J.: Jason Aronson Inc., 1987), p. xxxiii.

Acknowledgments

I would like to express my deep appreciation to the following people: My sister Deborah, for the hours she spent helping me with the research for this book. My sister Constance, for finding the time in her busy life to proofread the manuscript. Margie MacDonald and Sharon Creeden, for all their encouragement and advice, and for sending some interesting story variants my way. My husband Thom, who always came to my aid with his computer expertise, no matter how late the hour. My daughter Eleanor, who eagerly ate up my apples from heaven, even before I could polish them up to share with the general public. The librarians of King County, Seattle, and Snohomish Public Library Systems, who were so helpful in tracking down stray apples. My publisher and editor Diantha C. Thorpe and her husband and partner James Thorpe III, for their belief in *Apples from Heaven* when it was no more than a seed in this storyteller's heart. And, of course, this book could never have been written had I not been able to reap the heavenly harvest of those storytellers who have gone before.

Multicultural Index

Italic page numbers designate proverbs.